MISSING IN MYANMAR

JANE ELLYSON

A catalogue record for this book is available from the National Library of Australia.

ISBN: 978-0-6451358-0-0 (Paperback)
ISBN: 978-0-6451358-1-7 (ebook)

Editor: Jackie Bates

Cover Design by Nabinkarna on Fiverr

Cover photo taken by Matan Levanon

Map of Thailand and Myanmar by scrollavezza on fiverr

www.janeellyson.com

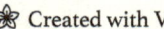 Created with Vellum

MAP OF MYANMAR AND THAILAND

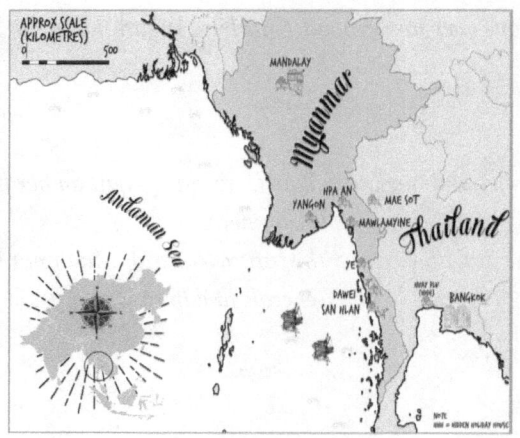

PROLOGUE

rabi, Thailand – January

Scott's kiss goodbye at Krabi airport had made Charlotte weak at the knees. It was a fitting end to a wonderful week of snorkelling and snuggling up around a fire on the beach. Many events looked forward to in life failed to meet expectations, but not this time. She and Scott had spent the week talking, among other things. She was still thinking about the *other things* when her phone rang, breaking her reverie-like state.

'How are you enjoying Thailand, Charlotte?' asked Teal. Charlotte was not in the least surprised that Teal Dubois knew where she was.

'It's been wonderful.'

'Do you mind staying in Southeast Asia a little longer? I've a job for you. Someone important is missing in Myanmar.

GOING ON RETREAT - JANUARY 29

C harlotte had known this day would come, even though she'd never actually said yes. But then she'd never said no. Her silence had been embraced by Teal Dubois as agreement to undertake an occasional assignment for the Australian Security Intelligence Organisation. In return, they would financially support her recently established fabric importing and design business, which she was delighted to name Chic Charlie. She was excited and nervous in equal measure at being given her first assignment.

The skills needed to become a spy were not a consideration when she'd struggled to decide between studying fashion or social media at Queensland University of Technology. One competency she'd acquired in good measure of late, was that of deception. She didn't like lying, but then she needed to do it so that her parents, and now boyfriend Scott, yes, she could call him that, weren't anxious. She could see that long-term, this gig would be difficult to maintain if she wanted to sustain close relationships. Still, the role had allowed her to break up an international slave trading network, facilitate the capture of a mobster and to meet some pretty interesting people.

As she hailed a tuk-tuk to take her back to the resort near the beach in Krabi, her thoughts turned to the next lie. She'd need an excuse to cover a week to possibly ten day absence. Miranda was currently so loved-up with Mason that she'd barely miss her. Her parents and Scott would require a trickier conversation.

'Hi Miranda. I'm back,' Charlotte called out loudly as she entered their room, in case her best friend was in an intimate situation with Scott's best friend Mason. The shower was running and Miranda was belting out a tortured, but passionate version of 'I've Been Writing Love Songs' by Daryl Braithwaite. Charlotte started collecting her clothes from the wardrobe.

'Did he get off OK?' Miranda asked from beneath the white towel that she was rubbing vigorously over her blonde bob.

'Yep. On his way to Singapore with a connection this evening to Port Vila in Vanuatu.'

'And when are you going to see each other again?'

'Don't know.'

'What? You two. Aren't you now officially in a relationship?'

'Yes. But it's complicated.' Miranda groaned. Charlotte continued, ignoring her, 'We both have careers taking off in different directions. I've got a lot to think about and I've decided I need time on my own to figure it out. I've booked a flight up north and I'm going on a mindfulness silent retreat for ten days. With the added bonus of not feeling like a gooseberry around you and Mason.'

'You're so full of surprises. I wouldn't have picked you as a silent retreat type.'

'Well, I'm not entirely sure I'll enjoy it, but it'll definitely be a new experience and who knows what I'll learn about myself.'

'Are you telling me the truth, C?'

'Mostly. I rarely feel like a gooseberry around you and Mason. Just so thrilled for you both.' Miranda gave her friend one of those hugs where you rock from side to side while squeezing.

'You must tell me all about it when you get back.'

'Well only if I'm allowed to. There are rules around participation in the retreat.'

'Are you really sure you want to go? Miranda asked.

'Not entirely.' Charlotte's phone pinged interrupting the conversation. 'Directions to the retreat,' she said putting her phone in her luggage. 'I'll say bye to Mason and be off. See you both at Don Muang airport in ten days.'

The earth below was scorched and dusty as the plane came into land at Mae Sot International Airport. It had clearly been a while since there was rain. Charlotte packed away her earphones, having listened to introductory Burmese on the flight from Krabi. She was chuffed to see a driver holding up a sign that read 'Chic Charlie'. Chic Charlie was the name of her fabric importing and fashion design house. It had been in operation for two months, but it still didn't feel real, even though she'd been busy sourcing fabrics from around the world. Her new business had been financially supported by a special government grant facilitated by Teal Dubois. Teal Dubois' official job title was Director, International Treaties. Her unofficial job title was recruiter of intelligence officers for the Australian Security Intelligence Organisation. Charlotte had met her when she had been caught up in an international slave trafficking syndicate in Italy. This hadn't been the first time she'd inadvertently ended up in the wrong place at the wrong time. She'd also managed to get kidnapped while impersonating a princess in Monaco. In both cases she'd managed to extricate herself with only minor injuries, attracting the attention of the international espionage community.

She turned her phone on again as she hopped into the taxi. There were five messages:

Message from Scott. *Cooling my heels in Singapore Airport. Can't stop thinking about last night.* ❤

Message from her mother. *Couldn't find the retreat you are going to online. Can you send us the link, just in case we need to contact you? Hugs.* 😊

Message from Miranda. *You left your hat behind.*

Message from Mason. *If you end up in any interesting situations, I wanna be the first person you call.*

Message from Teal. *Welcome to Mae Sot*

Charlotte smiled and looked out the taxi's window as a huge truck precariously overtook them on a double line. The taxi driver swerved off into the verge and then quickly recovered, a manoeuvre he'd clearly undertaken before. There were a few cyclists who hadn't been so lucky and had taken a tumble. Charlotte watched through the back window as they dusted themselves off and remounted their bicycles. Relieved they were OK and annoyed that her driver had not stopped, she started texting.

Message to Scott. *Keep thinking those good thoughts.*

Message to Miranda. *Unlikely to need hat.*

Message to Mason. *Do you ever stop being a features writer for Hello? Can't for the life of me think that there will be anything glamorous to report at the retreat. But if there is, of course, I will reach out to my favourite journo.*

Teal waved as the taxi pulled into the car park of the J2 Hotel. The taxi driver pulled her luggage from the trunk. Even though the humidity was climbing, Teal's short grey hair was perfectly coiffed.

'You've met Dang then?' Teal asked. Charlotte was aware that barely a word had passed between the dangerous driver Dang and herself on the short trip from the airport as she had been pre-occupied texting.

'Well not properly. Nice to meet you, Dang,' Charlotte offered holding out her hand.

'Nice to meet you too Miss Wyatt.'

'Charlotte, please Dang,'

'Of course.'

'Dang is not actually a driver by profession,' Teal said. Why does that not surprise me Charlotte thought to herself. 'He's actually a librarian,' Teal continued.

'Goodness. How wonderful. I love reading,' Charlotte blurted out. It sounded like a superficial thing to say. She chastised herself as she dropped her bag in her room and joined Teal and Dang in the dining room for a refreshing watermelon juice. The three of them were alone.

'First priority,' Teal announced, 'apply for a visa for Myanmar. You can do that online and it will be issued within the hour. Second priority. Send this web link and phone number to whoever in your immediate circle is likely to try and contact you while you're on assignment.' Charlotte looked-up the link and smiled.

'Wow, I would really like to visit this retreat.'

'Maybe next time. And third priority. If there's any hint that the military is about to take control, head for the border. Here's a list of our safe houses. You will need to memorize and then destroy this list.'

'Gotcha. And my mission is?'

'To find and extract Maiah Thar Khin. She's an inspiring young leader in the National League for Democracy and she's gone missing. She may be hiding, or she may have been arrested. She needs to be under international protection. The future of Myanmar demands it.'

'And you think I can do this?'

'You've shown yourself to be extremely agile and inventive. This is a core requirement for an IO.' Charlotte guessed that IO meant intelligence officer. 'Dang here will manage your induction, and he'll be your driver throughout the assignment. Wear this watch. It will allow us to communicate if the internal communications systems are shut down. It will also be the most effective way for you to file your daily reports,' Charlotte nodded. 'You should also wear one of these shirts at all times. They have an inbuilt tracker and a fabric like chain mail, which will resist a knife or a bullet. Mind you, it will still hurt a lot if you get shot. Now these sunglasses will allow you to take videos and for us to see what you see. The manual controls are here on the arms, and they can also be voice activated. We can also talk to you through the arms. The sunglasses are unbreakable and also very good at blocking out the sun.'

'And where's my Aston Martin?' Charlotte asked. Teal raised her eyebrows.

'Don't be ridiculous Charlotte. Who do you think you are? James Bond? You would be picked up by military police within thirty seconds of driving an ostentatious vehicle like that.'

'Just joking! This is a little bit exciting,' she replied with obvious understatement.

'Remember – you've been chosen because of your capacity for getting out of tricky situations with the barest of resources. These tools can help.'

'Understood. So how do I start the search?'

'We have an officer embedded in a United Nations taskforce currently working in Hpa-an. As luck would have it, they're in Mae Sot this afternoon for a regional meeting. They always stop for refreshments at the

Mixirista café in the main street. Make sure you're there and our agent will reach out to you.'

'Anything else?'

'Make sure you buy fabric samples along the way. It will help to maintain your cover.'

'If you insist.'

Charlotte ordered a banana smoothie and took a seat in the corner of the café. There were several well-dressed Europeans already seated around a large table with their laptops open, engaged in serious conversation. No-one seemed interested in her. She finished her drink and walked over to the counter to order a green tea cake. On the way back she picked up a magazine and flicked through it while she ate the cake. Thirty minutes passed and no one so much as threw her a glance. The meeting concluded and all the foreigners left. Charlotte checked her messages and felt that she was now very obvious with neither drink nor food in front of her. She walked slowly to the door and stepped out into the hot evening. No-one was outside waiting for her. She walked slowly along the street, looking for anyone who might be her contact. A tuk-tuk driver was sitting cross-legged in the back of his vehicle, with a small suitcase of amulets resting in front of him, clearly for sale to those walking by. Charlotte stopped to admire these small, good luck charms.

'Come and have a closer look,' said a familiar voice from the back seat of the tuk-tuk. It was Dang.

'This is my friend Amin. He's a driver for the UN folk who are in town for the conference. His family has a new fabric manufacturing business near Hpa-an that you might like to visit.'

'Yes. I'd like that very much,' Charlotte said taking the card from him. She wasn't sure what to make of Amin. Was he her contact? Why hadn't he met her inside as had been arranged? She bade the two men goodbye and walked back to the hotel. As she entered, the receptionist called out to her.

'I have a message for you.' Charlotte unfolded the piece of paper which said,

Take the 5:00pm river cruise tomorrow evening in Hpa-an

Charlotte was confused and didn't know whether she should trust the message. Teal had departed for Chiang Rai in northern Thailand, and she didn't want to bother her unless it was important. And Dang had behaved strangely too. She popped the message in her pocket and went to her room to pack her things. There were messages on her phone from Miranda and her mum. She resisted the urge to respond, after all, she was meant to be on a ten day no-communication retreat. This might be the hardest part of the spy gig.

There was a knock on her door. It was Dang.

'Come,' he said simply. 'You need to learn self-defence.' Charlotte was irritated by his assumption that she had no skills in this area. Scott had shown her several ways to break free from a tight hold and she had demonstrated rather effective skills. she thought, in both France and Sicily, escaping from both a boat and a helicopter.

Men. Still, she recognised that a refresher course was probably a good idea.

Dang's training session was more comprehensive and brutal than anything Scott had shown her and she hoped she'd never have to burst someone's eye or break their neck. Every time Dang put his arms around her in a hold, she thought of Scott.

'Very good,' he said at last. 'Now I'll show you how to use those tools Teal gave you.'

Over dinner that evening, they relaxed a little in each other's company. Dang shared a little about his family and Charlotte did the same. Dang was Burmese and like his father, had married a Thai. While they lived in Mae Sot in Thailand, he frequently travelled home to Dawei in southern Myanmar where his parents lived. He loved books and would have preferred to have spent his life as a librarian. There were limited prospects for librarians in Myanmar, but with excellent written and spoken English, he could tutor children while driving taxis for foreigners. Charlotte sensed that there was more to his back story, so she too chose to be selective in what she shared with him. She was happy to reveal that she was an only child, had finished studying fashion the previous year and had now set up a fabric and design shop in Brisbane. She told him about her brief foray into modelling and that she'd met Teal at a party on a yacht in Rome.

'And what do you think of your government,' he asked. Charlotte was surprised by the sudden turn in the direction of the conversation.

'I don't have too much of an opinion at this stage,' she replied honestly.

'Then that is your privilege,' he replied curtly. He

stood and announced that he would be in the car park to collect her at 7:00am the following morning.

In her room, Charlotte reviewed her messages.

Message from Teal. *Do you have the information you need?*

Message from her mother. *I still don't have the contact details for your retreat.*

Message from Scott. *Just about to board my flight. Will call you from Port Vila if I can. Thinking about you. All the time.* 🖤🖤🤍

Message to Teal. *Doubt it. Lucky I'm good at winging it. More from Hpa-an.*

Message to her mother. *Here's the number for the resort. Emergency contact only. Turning my phone off now.*

Message to Scott. *Keep thinking about me because every time you do, I'll be thinking about you.*

2

CROSSING THE BORDER - JANUARY 30

Dang was in the car park at seven the following morning, sitting in a white Toyota Hilux. Charlotte threw her bag into the back of the utility beside half a dozen boxes.

'What's in the boxes?' she asked.

'Books.'

'Of course,' she replied. They listened to the local radio as they drove to the border.

'What are they saying?'

'It's uncertain in Myanmar. Many whispers.'

Charlotte felt apprehensive as they joined a long queue of vehicles including trucks and motorcycles. She was also surprised to see a troop of cyclists, the same cyclists that Dang had caused to tumble on the main road into Mae Sot the previous day.

'You go this way as a foreigner,' Dang instructed, pointing to the left. 'You show them your visa and I see you on the other side of the river.' Charlotte joined the queue behind the foreign cyclists.

Two hours later, with a stamp in her passport, she

walked across the Thai-Myanmar Friendship Bridge and into bedlam. There were vehicles overburdened with goods, honking their horns energetically, trying to get on their way. It was hard to spot Dang's truck as there were so many of the same make and colour. A loud whistle caught her attention and she spotted Dang fifty metres down the road, emerging from a small shop, carrying several bottles of water.

It was a long and bumpy ride to Hpa-an. They shared the road with many military trucks full of soldiers. Their bored stares were a little unnerving. They had to stop at Kayin State checkpoints where Charlotte's passport was again scrutinised. The radio played for the entire trip. Dang alternated between stations with news analysis or rock music. She was sure it was a tactic for limiting conversation. The eerily beautiful Zwegabin mountains suddenly appeared through the dust in the distance.

'Sacred mountains to Kayin people. Hpa-an not far now,' Dang announced. 'First we go to the factory.'

'How will visiting the factory help us find Maiah?'

'Is an important part of your cover. And is something you'd like I think. Very beautiful fabrics.'

'OK,' she replied hesitantly. 'But I'm a little unnerved by the military presence on the roads. I've not been here before and perhaps this is normal, but I find it unsettling. A bit like thunder warning of an approaching storm.'

'You have good instincts. A storm is approaching.'

The gentle hum of sewing machines could be heard as they entered the factory that had the feel of an aircraft hangar. There were twenty women, their faces painted with thanaka paste, sitting at desks in four rows. There was a high ceiling and low hanging fans and hundreds of rolls of beautifully coloured silk fabric. The women were making traditional sarongs, longyis and eingyis. The supervisor immediately called one of the women up to measure Charlotte.

'Thank you. I don't have time. We leave tomorrow.'

'It will be ready by then.' As the woman took multiple measurements, Charlotte watched Dang quietly slip into a small room away from the main factory floor. With the measurements completed she was then shown a myriad of fabrics to choose between. This was such a difficult task as they were all magnificent. She made her choices and tried without success to pay. *Mr Dang will take care of it,* she was told.

'Thank you,' she said as she left them to find Dang. They were talking Burmese so what they were saying wasn't clear, but there was visible disagreement. They hushed when Charlotte entered.

'My apologies for interrupting. Dang, I need to get to the departure point for the cruise. Should I take a...,' she hesitated not knowing what public transport would be best.

'Of course not. We leave now.'

Charlotte was certain that the conversation she interrupted had been politically related. 'What did you learn?' she asked, deliberately ambiguous.

'More people have gone missing.'

'So why were you arguing?'

'We do not agree on what we should do next.'

'Did you learn anything useful that will help me in the search for Maiah?' He shook his head.

They drove into the centre of Hpa-an and left Charlotte's luggage at the Golden Palace Hotel before heading for the riverside.

'I'll meet you at the night market in two hours,' Dang said as he dropped her off.

The cruise boat was styled as a paddle steamer, without the paddles. The two decks were mainly full of tourists from Myanmar, although some of the foreign cyclists she'd last seen at the border were also aboard. Charlotte ordered a drink and took a seat near the rail. The sun was setting and the view over the distant Zwegabin mountains had an ethereal quality about it, with smoky hues of silver and pink. No one attempted to speak to her until the boat stopped at the bottom of a rocky plinth to allow everyone to watch the exit of tens of thousands of bats from caves deep in the mountain, in a floating ribbon across the sky that stretched for miles. What made the viewing even more spectacular was the dramatic dive bombing being undertaken by sea eagles into the ribbon of bats to grab their easy-picking dinner. Charlotte was so mesmerised by the scene that she initially didn't hear the person standing beside her speak.

'I said, one needs to be aware of enemies who appear suddenly at night.' Charlotte turned around startled. 'I'm Xavier. I left the message for you in Mae Sot. Come.' He led her to two seats at the back of the boat.

'What do you mean about enemies in the night?'

'OK. I was feeling a bit poetic watching those eagles munch on the bats. But I was also being serious. You need to be careful about who you trust. Let me tell you what I know. Maiah Thar Khin was last seen by one of our agents, five days ago in Mawlamyine. She'd given a speech for the National League for Democracy, which was broken up by the military, who took several people into custody, possibly including her. There have been no names released so we can't be sure. All our contacts have suddenly gone quiet.'

'So what should I do?'

'Go to Mawlamyine. There's a blue tea house where members of the National League for Democracy some-times congregate. You could also visit the Kyaik Than Lan Pagoda at 5:00pm. This is where the locals gather to watch the sunset over the Andaman Sea. You're unlikely to be arrested as it's a sacred place. Your driver Dang may have other suggestions. Take him with you.'

'To be honest with you, I'm not one hundred percent sure that I trust him.'

'He's all you have for now. Be on your guard.'

The night market was a short distance away from where the boat docked. Charlotte could see the twinkling lights hanging from electric poles, hear people chatting excit-edly and smell something delicious sizzling in the pan. As she strolled between the vendors, she was overwhelmed by the food choices and for a moment forgot that she was on assignment.

'Over here,' Dang called out. He pointed to a small plastic chair beside him around a large table where other diners were enjoying eating from shared bowls.

'Did you meet your contact?'

'Yes.'

'Did you learn where Maiah is?'

'No. Only where she was last seen in Mawlamyine. How long will it take to drive there?'

'It's not far. Maybe ninety minutes. It depends on checkpoints.'

'Good. We leave first thing tomorrow.' Dang was watching her carefully. Charlotte imagined that he was debating what to say to her next.

'What would you like to eat?' This was not the kind of question that Charlotte was expecting. They were both being careful.

'You choose.'

Dang nodded and spoke to the woman behind the cooking plate. Fifteen minutes later Charlotte was enjoying pork curry and tea leaf salad. While she ate, she watched the different family gatherings enjoying their time together. She felt a pang of homesickness and wondered what her parents were doing. Her thoughts also flicked to Scott. She'd like to bring him to this market beside the river. He'd probably already started his yacht race from Port Vila to Bundaberg.

Later that evening, after she'd texted a brief status report to Teal, she called Scott.

'Aren't you breaking the rules calling me from your retreat?'

'In more ways than you know.' They both laughed.

'Seriously. How's it going there?'

'It's quiet.'

'Isn't that what you wanted?'

'I guess. I've been thinking about you,' Charlotte said.

'And I've been thinking about you. I think that as soon as you've given your parents a hug in Brisbane in ten days' time, you should hotfoot it onto a plane to Hamilton Island to spend quality time with me. You could probably sell some of your fancy designs through the boutiques there, so it would be a combined business and pleasure trip. Oops, I meant leisure.'

'Nope. Pleasure and business sound wonderful. Let's discuss it more once I'm home.'

'Look forward to that. We're about to set sail. I don't expect to be contactable for a while. Keep safe.'

'You too.' A moments silence passed before they both whispered goodbye and rang off. Charlotte fell asleep dreaming of being on the yacht with Scott and sailing off into the sunset.

3

LEAVING HPA-AN - JANUARY 31

Charlotte was abruptly woken at 5:00am by the honking of horns from street traffic. She dressed and went for a walk outside, enjoying the cool of the morning. Dang was pulling into the garage with the truck as she arrived back at the hotel. She wondered where he had been at such an early hour.

'Here,' he said. 'Your clothes are finished.' Charlotte looked in the bag at the beautiful garments and hoped the ladies hadn't worked through the night to get them finished.

'These are so beautiful. Can you please tell them I love them?' Dang grinned momentarily, delighted with her response. A shadow then flickered across his face and his trademark seriousness returned.

'We need to go. There is not a good feeling today in Hpa-an. Are you ready?'

'I'll get my things,' Charlotte replied.

As they drove out of Hpa-an, two things began to be seen with increasing frequency. The first was trucks from the national army, lumbering along full of soldiers. Charlotte fiddled with her sunglasses and turned her recorder on so that Teal could see what she was seeing. The second were large canvas signs with images of Aung San Suu Kyi, and the message in English,

WE STAND WITH YOU.

Aung San Suu Kyi, the daughter of Myanmar's independence hero, General Aung San, had led the National League for Democracy (NLD) to victory in Myanmar's first openly contested election in twenty-five years. Ms Suu Kyi had spent nearly fifteen years in detention between 1989 and 2010. The tension between the military and Ms Suu Kyi was now beginning to break. She was seventy-five, now, and the need for younger leadership was apparent in the party and in the international community, which was why so many had high hopes for Maiah Thar Khin. Charlotte felt that the task of finding Maiah was beyond her ability. She realised she hadn't discussed with Teal a date to abandon the project, and made a mental note to mention this on their next call.

They entered the outskirts of Mawlamyine, the largest city in the state of Mon. Dang surprised Charlotte by stopping first at the town's university.

'What are we doing here?' she asked.

'Delivering the books I brought from Mae Sot.' Charlotte was a little bewildered but hopped out of the truck to help Dang carry one of the boxes inside the library. Several staff came out to greet Dang and then began chatting animatedly. Dang asked her to collect the last box while he continued with his discourse. When he finally returned to the truck Charlotte asked what they had been discussing.

'They were thrilled to receive the books.'

'Anything about where Maiah might be?' Dang was a little taken aback by the question.

'No. They're just librarians.'

'I would personally never underestimate a librarian. They know where to find things, like information and people.'

He regarded her carefully. 'Where have you been told to go in Mawlamyine?'

'To a blue tea house. Do you know it?'

'Yes. It's not far from the Than Lwin Seesar Hotel where you will stay tonight.'

'You won't be staying there?'

'No. I have friends in Mawlamyine.'

'The librarians?'

'And others.' He was clearly not interested in divulging more than was necessary. He dropped her at the front of the hotel, letting her know he'd be back in an hour to take her to the tea house.

The Than Lwin Seesar Hotel had a reassuringly large bright yellow generator out front. After throwing her bag on the bed she walked up the stairs to the top floor from where she enjoyed a wonderful view across the Andaman Sea. There were three large tankers, a medical ship as identified by a large red cross, and a dozen smaller boats sitting patiently in the calm water. She looked at her watch and could see she had time to explore the local area before Dang returned. She turned right then right again from the hotel and passed a motorcycle repair shop, with two goats tethered out front, and then several fish and chicken markets. As she rushed across a busy road, she spotted a bright blue building, with men sitting around small tables. She went inside, took a seat at a long table and ordered tea.

'You should try the samosas as well,' came a voice with a familiar Australian accent. 'They're delicious.'

'Thank you, I will,' Charlotte replied. 'Where are you from?'

'Sydney. And yourself?'

'Brisbane.'

'Tourist?'

'No. Fabric merchant. Here on a sourcing tour.'

'And you?'

'Professor at the local university. And why did you choose this teahouse today?'

'Because it was recommended to me. And you?'

'Because I was told I'd find the founder of Chic Charlie here, and that she'd value my recommendations on places where she could source interesting products.' They both smiled, relieved to have found each other. Professor Shane Tiell had last seen Maiah two weeks previously when she'd spoken to his students about the need for democratic reform. It had been a wonderful speech and the students were inspired by this young leader. He was aware that there were rumours that she'd gone missing. From her presentation to his class, he knew that she had family in the village of Mudon which was half an hour's drive south of the city. He expressed concern about the increasing number of military trucks on the roads and hoped she was lying low with family members.

'Where should I look for her in the village?' Charlotte asked.

'Start at the blackboard maker's shop. He knows everyone.'

'They still have blackboard makers in Myanmar?'

'Unfortunately, yes. Change is coming slowly.'

Dang was waiting for her in the hotel lobby when she returned.

'I want to go to the village of Mudon this morning.'

'What about the tea house?'

'I've already been.'

'Without me?' he blurted out.

'Yes. It was not my intention. I found it be chance,' she replied, surprised by his defensive outburst.

'What did you learn?' he demanded.

'Not very much, which is why we need to go to Mudon.'

A strange mood settled in the cab of the Hilux as they drove to Mudon. Neither spoke, each wary of the other. Dang parked and followed Charlotte into the blackboard maker's shop on the main road. The small blackboards hanging on the wall were charming, belonging to a different era. Charlotte selected three and passed them to the man sitting on the floor with a saw.

'May I buy these?' The man smiled, took her money and put her purchases in a paper bag. 'Can you help me with something,' Charlotte started, hoping the man spoke English. 'I'm looking for the house of the Thar Khin family.' The man appeared to understand the question, but was startled by it. He had a rapid conversation with Dang in Burmese.

'Please tell me what he is saying,' Charlotte implored.

'Maiah's father died yesterday. She's in mourning supporting her mother.

'Oh, I see.'

'I do not think it is appropriate we visit,' he said.

'I won't stay long. I just want to check that she's fine, then I'll feel I've completed the assignment, and we can go back to Thailand.' Dang nodded.

There were two puppies playing in the dirt at the front of the double story timber cottage with a distinctive blue, green and yellow glass spirit house at the side. The confident way Dang drove into the area in front of the house was a clear sign to Charlotte that he'd been here before. Her suspicions were confirmed when several children ran out of the house and jumped into his arms. A young woman, with round eyes, long straight hair and a welcoming smile walked out of the house.

'Back so soon Dang? And I assume this is Charlotte Wyatt, who's here to rescue me.' Charlotte laughed.

'Yes, that would be me. You knew where she was all the time, didn't you Dang?'

He nodded.

'Come inside for tea and we can talk.'

It didn't take long for Charlotte to realise why this engaging young woman had been identified as a future leader. She was well educated, articulate and passionate about driving positive change in Myanmar. After tea, she took Charlotte on a tour of local businesses including a rubber band factory, hat factory with a variety of models made from bamboo leaves, and a rope factory with products made from coconut fibres. Charlotte was delighted when they stopped at a market where a woman was selling a wonderful array of sarongs and longyis. It was difficult limiting her purchases to only six swathes of the beautiful fabric.

While they walked, they talked. Maiah's father had passed a week before. She had been with him during his last days and had been supporting her mother since. He had been proud of her political aspirations, but made her promise that she would be careful in speaking out. She struggled with what this promise meant as it was difficult to drive change without taking risks.

'Well, it seems to me that many people in the local and international community are motivated for you to succeed. Don't hesitate to reach out for help.'

'I will, and thank you for coming to check that I was safe.'

It was late afternoon before Dang dropped her off at the hotel in Mawlamyine. They agreed to leave the following morning at 7:00 for Mae Sot and he encouraged her to walk up the hill to watch the sun setting from the Kyaik Than Lan Pagoda. There were many visitors walking slowly and respectfully through the complex. No-one looked at her and the only person who spoke with her was a guard reminding her to remove her socks. It was a beautiful place to watch the end of the day with the sun bouncing off the golden peaks of the pagoda. Darkness came quickly as she walked back to the hotel. What an amazing trip, Charlotte thought to herself. She pulled her phone out and sent Teal a text message.

Message to Teal. *Pleased to report that Maiah has been found near Mawlamyine. She's safe and well. Dang and I will be returning to Thailand tomorrow.*

Message from Teal. *Good work! Thank you.*

Charlotte admired her new purchases as she packed her bag. She planned to make skirts for her mother and Miranda and wondered which fabrics they would choose from among this beautiful selection. All was good in her world as she drifted off to sleep.

4

ONE MINUTE PAST TWELVE - FEBRUARY 1

Charlotte slept soundly until the air-conditioning went off at midnight. She reached for the light switches which weren't working. Moments later the hotel's generator kicked in and light flooded her room. There was shouting on the streets below and she ran up the interior stairs to the roof to identify the source of the disturbance. A few people were shouting but she didn't understand what they were saying. One of the hotel staff joined her on the roof terrace.

'What's happened?' Charlotte asked.

'Aung San Suu Kyi has gone missing and we think that the military are staging a coup.'

Charlotte returned to her room. The internet was down, but there was a message on her watch from Teal.

Hold tight. We are monitoring the situation. More instructions tomorrow.

She crawled back under the covers and had a fitful night's sleep, wondering, how safe the world would be tomorrow and what her new instructions would be. The internet was still down when she heard the 5:00am calls to prayer. There was a new message on her watch from Teal.

Situation uncertain. Many missing. Maiah to be extracted to Thailand.

Charlotte checked the BBC news website on her watch.

Southeast Asia correspondent, Jonathan Head, reported that the armed forces in Myanmar have confirmed that they have carried out a coup d'etat, their first against a civilian government since 1962. This was in apparent violation of the constitution which the military had promised to honour.

A weary looking Dang was in the hotel's reception at 6:30.

'Did you get any sleep?' He shook his head. 'Where's Maiah?'

'She's safe.' Charlotte noted that he had avoided answering her question.

'Did you receive Teal's direction?'

'No. I'm only the driver.' Charlotte noted the resentment in his reply.

'She wants us to get Maiah across the border to Thailand. To safety.'

'Of course she does. That will be difficult as the military are looking for her, but more importantly, because

Maiah does not want to leave Myanmar.' Charlotte suddenly understood why Dang had been so evasive. He did not support the agency's objectives for removing Maiah to Thailand to keep her safe.

There were two bicycles in the back of the Hilux and a large tarpaulin. Charlotte put her bag in the back of the utility and glanced under the tarpaulin. Maiah gave her a wave. Dang drove for half an hour on the main road, before turning on to a dirt track. Travel was slow and nerve racking because of the number of military vehicles overtaking them. They finally stopped at a market beside a temple when a troop of cyclists were eating breakfast.

'I met the leader of this group last night on the Walking Street in Mawlamyine. Nice man. He's agreed that you both can join them today. You will be safe. The military will not be looking for Maiah with a group of foreigners. I will pick you up at the cemetery in Thanbyuzat.'

'And hopefully we will be alive,' Charlotte replied. Dang did not know what to make of her comment. 'And where will we go from there?'

'I'm working on it,' he replied. 'I'll see you this afternoon.' Maiah and Charlotte said goodbye and introduced themselves to the cycling troop, before joining them in eating nan gyi thoke, a thick curry noodle salad, for breakfast. They were grateful that there were few questions about who they were and where they were going.

Charlotte enjoyed the ride alongside the coast. It was good to be off the main road and in the countryside. It felt safe. They passed through small villages where immaculately dressed children in long sarongs with crisp white shirts were riding their bicycles to school. After two hours of cycling, they arrived in a small fishing village where arrangements had been made to transport the cyclists to Kyaikkhami via three large fishing boats.

The internet was still down, but Charlotte could see from the news on her watch that many people were withdrawing cash from automatic tellers all over the country, in expectation of a cash crunch. The multi-national cycling troop did not appear to be aware of the seriousness of the political machinations taking place. This was a good thing, Charlotte reasoned. Her watch beeped indicating the arrival of a message from Teal.

Message from Teal. *Is Maiah with you?*

Message to Teal. *Yes.*

Message from Teal. *Good work. More soon.*

Charlotte was relieved that that was all Teal asked of her.

The boat journey was cramped but pleasant. Charlotte slept most of the way and felt rejuvenated by the time the boat pulled up beside a long rocky pier. They worked together to remove the bikes and panniers and to carry them up to solid ground. They enjoyed a drink in the shade and Charlotte googled the town on her watch. She learnt that Kyaikkham had for a short period being the capital of British Lower Burma, before the responsibility was taken over by Mawlamyine. It was difficult to imagine how important this town had once been, as it was largely deserted today. Charlotte was pleased about that.

After a quick break for lunch they remounted their bikes. It was the hottest part of the day and Maiah was struggling to keep up. Charlotte rode with her at the back of the troop, offering encouragement. They were pleased to see Dang's truck parked out the front of the Thanbyuzayat prisoner of war cemetery when they arrived two hours later. They waved goodbye to the cycling troop who were spending the night in Thanbyuzayt. It took another two hours to drive to a monastery at a sacred place near Ye called Banana Mountain. They were ushered inside a house at the top of the site. Maiah was clearly suffering from heat exhaustion. Charlotte encouraged her to drink lots of water and rest. She walked outside to join Dang, who was enjoying the cool evening breeze while taking in the spectacular view.

'I think we should stay for a day or two until Maiah has fully recovered.'

'I agree,' Dang replied.

'Well, that's a first,' Charlotte quipped. 'Hopefully we can find even more common ground tomorrow.'

5

BANANA MOUNTAIN

A rooster outside her window announced the arrival of the new day, several times. The rooster didn't understand that they were very early. Charlotte rolled over and looked at the news on her watch. The BBC was reporting that in major cities and towns, troops were now patrolling the streets and a night-time curfew had been introduced. The military had also declared a one-year state of emergency and announced replacements for a number of ministerial positions. Charlotte also looked at the message from Teal.

Message from Teal. *It's imperative to get Maiah out. Not only for her own safety but for the future of Myanmar.*

Message to Teal. *Message understood.*

It was an easy way to respond without responding.

Maiah was sitting at a table in the kitchen talking animatedly with Dang. It was clear from her voice tone and body posture that she was fully recovered from cycling in the heat the previous day.

'Morning. Thank you for looking after me last night.'

'My pleasure. Great to see that you've got your strength back.'

'It's back up,' Dang cried out looking at his phone. Maiah and Dang spent a few minutes reading their messages, until the internet went down again.'

'Good news. The President of the United States has raised the threat of sanctions and both the UN and UK are condemning the coup. We have international support. We need to rally the people to resist. Our collective power will be our strength.'

'As long as you're not arrested,' Charlotte said.

'Yes. This is something I need to avoid,' Maiah replied matter-of-factly.

'So, what's the plan?' Charlotte asked.

'We wait until the sun comes up then we drive to Dawei. It should only take four hours, but that depends on the number of military checkpoints and of the need to take an alternate route. Dang can drop me at a safe house and then take you to the border at Htee Kee. That will take another five to six hours from Dawei. You should be safely back in Thailand this evening.'

Charlotte walked back to her room to gather her things. She put on the shirt Teal had given her and sent her another text message.

Message to Teal. *Please obtain information on military movements today.*

Message from Teal. *Understood.*

Charlotte took her second special shirt to Maiah in the kitchen.

'This is a lucky shirt for you, provided by my company. I think you should wear it today.'

As they drove down from Banana Mountain at daybreak, Charlotte was in awe of the huge ,golden buddhas sitting serenely, back-to-back on the hill. She hoped that one day she could come back to this tranquil place with Scott. And suddenly all her thoughts were of him. It would not be too long now until they were together again.

6

DRIVE TO DAWEI

The road south was quieter than usual. Charlotte's watch beeped every time a military vehicle was within 500 metres. They all held their breath as what was inevitably a large truck, approached and then passed. The road became busier as the morning wore on. Potholes littered the main road, making it impossible to drive faster than 60 kilometres an hour. Additionally, there were often no verges, with a steep drop into a valley on one side. It was extremely difficult to overtake but this did not stop a number of impatient drivers from trying. They stopped at the checkpoint on the border between Mon State and the Tanintharyi region. Maiah was instantly recognised, the guard smiled and they were quickly waved through. It was only the national military that were looking to find and contain her.

Charlotte's watch detected a significant convoy of military vehicles up ahead, so the decision was made to attempt to drive around them via the narrow paths between rice fields. This proved problematic and they were soon stuck in a wet bog waiting on an irritated farmer to pull them out with his tractor.

They finally joined the main road and drove slowly towards a large checkpoint. They quickly agreed on a strategy. Dang explained that he was employed as a driver for this foreign businesswoman sourcing fabrics for her business. His wife was their interpreter and they were driving her today to the border with Thailand. The guard asked about the reason for the two bicycles, which were easily explained as a chance to combine business with pleasure. The guard nodded, waved them on and then went into the small hut to report to his supervisor. They were only a short distance along the road when they could hear a shout and see a guard waving at them in the windscreen mirror for them to come back. Dang put his foot to the floor, and took off as bullets started hitting the chassis. Charlotte looked at her watch and directed Dang to turn right at Kaleinaung where there was an alternate and slower road into Dawei. More importantly, there were currently no military vehicles travelling on it, according to the satellite images on Charlotte's watch.

It was late afternoon when they finally arrived in Dawei. They were nervous when they drove into town but their bullet riddled truck passed unnoticed. Dang parked the truck at the back of the safe house to avoid detection and they went inside to join a dozen other people sharing what information they had gathered. They learnt that Aung San Suu Kyi had been detained and charged with breaching import and export laws. Her whereabouts were unclear. There was universal support for the resistance movement, to be indicated by the wearing of red or black ribbons and by using a three-finger salute. More boldly, they planned to bang on saucepans at eight o'clock that evening. This was a well-known practice to ward off evil and the meaning to the junta was clear. Maiah was adamant that she wanted to give a public speech to inspire townsfolk to be brave and to continue resisting. Dang tried reasoning with her but Charlotte could see from her body language that he was not successful in getting her to change her mind.

Eight o'clock arrived and the banging of pans and the honking of horns reverberated across town. It was an inspiring sound and everyone on the street with their improvised drums, had a look of determination.

A car park in front of a central hotel had been chosen as the rendezvous point. A small crowd of six quickly blossomed to sixty. Dang and Charlotte welcomed people as they arrived and kept their eyes on the road for the arrival of military. Charlotte watched Maiah's speech with wonder. While she couldn't understand the words, she could feel the passion. When the general's men arrived in three large trucks, the crowd stood defiantly around Maiah, blocking her from their reach. Then a Mexican wave rippled across the crowd as they held up their three fingered show of defiance. One of the uniformed men started addressing the crowd through a loudspeaker. From his clenched fist it was clear that he was telling the crowd to disperse and go home. They ignored him and started banging their saucepans, staring down their enemy. For five minutes there was a standoff. A whistle suddenly sounded and the military men climbed back into their vehicles and drove away to the loud cheers of the crowd.

Members of the crowd filed towards Maiah to thank her. Charlotte was in awe of Maiah and the inspirational power she had over her community of followers. The streets were quiet as they walked back to the safe house.

Dang suddenly stopped and turned around. He was listening. There was the gentle rumble of an approaching truck.

'The military are coming back. Run.' Charlotte grabbed Maiah's hand and dragged her down a narrow lane while Dang continued running down the main street, shouting in an effort to draw attention away from his colleagues. Charlotte pulled Maiah behind a fence and forced her to squat.

'I don't want to hide from them,' Maiah whispered.

'And I don't want you to be captured,' Charlotte replied tersely. A dog started barking in the house behind them, revealing where they were hiding. They stood up slowly, then walked quietly out onto the narrow lane and directly into the arms of the military.

CONTAINED

Being arrested was a new experience for Charlotte. It was also a very surreal one as it was happening in a foreign language. Maiah was a competent translator, advising Charlotte that their crimes included breaching the night curfew and encouraging a gathering of more than four people. They were taken to Dawei jail where their possessions were taken from them and a note made in a register which they were both required to sign. Her watch was viewed suspiciously and *accidentally* broken through the checking process, but Charlotte knew that the trackers inside their shirts would be sending out location details to Teal.

They were taken to a dormitory shared with four others. The other women were excited at their arrival. They all knew who Maiah was and asked for news from the outside. The lights started flickering, a sign that they were about to be turned off. Charlotte said good night to the other women and climbed up onto her bunk bed. Her mind was working in overdrive. What should they do next? Wait to be rescued or look for opportunities to rescue themselves? She was pretty sure that Maiah would be happy to stay put, recognising the power of being arrested. She on the other hand, had no intention of languishing in jail. Tomorrow she'd consider her options. For now, she needed to sleep. There was a tiny window the size of a hand above her bed through which she could see the full moon. She wondered if Scott would be looking at the moon at that very moment and thinking about her. Boy, he'd be cranky if he knew she was in jail. The thought made her smile as she drifted off to sleep.

A rat scurrying across the centre of the room woke her. The other girls were already awake and visiting the bathroom. One of the girls looked at her, smiled and said hello. This was unexpected. A few of the younger girls had a smattering of English and were pleased by the opportunity to practice it. Charlotte didn't know what the time was when all the doors to the dormitories were unlocked. All the prisoners politely filed into a large room, collecting a mug of tea and a bowl of rice in broth from the kitchens serving window, before sitting down at communal tables. Charlotte surveyed the room, looking for exits, and wondered about the rest of the jail. Maiah was laughing with some of the other inmates. This annoyed Charlotte a little as she felt that they should both be focussing on how to get out.

'Guess what's happening tomorrow night?' Charlotte had no idea how to respond to this question. 'They're having a fashion parade. And they are so excited to learn that you are a fashion designer and former model.'

'Words fail me, Maiah. This is so surreal. Why? Why on earth are they having a fashion parade, and what clothes are they going to wear? I hardly think that our current outfits are runway worthy.'

'It was the idea of the prison warden. Visitors have been stopped of late because of the virus. So to cheer everybody up, they've arranged for a runway to be built in the central courtyard, and everyone gets to strut their stuff.'

'But you and I don't have outfits?'

'There's some material left over from the other prisoners' outfits. It may have to be a patchwork look. Why are you looking so grumpy? How else were you planning on spending your time today?' Charlotte had of course imagined that she'd be safely back in Thailand today, with this espionage adventure behind her. She was irritated by Maiah's lack of focus on examining how to get out of the jail. It was almost as if she was settling in for the long haul.

A guard came into the mess hall, interrupting their conversation, and pointed at Charlotte. Maiah asked the guard what she wanted.

'You have a visitor,' Maiah reported. Surprised, Charlotte stood up and pointed at Maiah. The guard shook her finger. Only Charlotte was to accompany the guard. She was taken to a small room where she was patted down in the presence of another woman.

'How your people know you here?' the guard asked accusingly in broken English. Charlotte hesitated.

'The sky. There are satellites in the sky with big eyes.' The response seemed to satisfy the woman.

A well-dressed, largish woman with short auburn hair, black square glasses and large gold-looped earrings was sitting on the other side of the table in a room designated for supervised conversations. A large piece of Perspex was secured in the centre of the table to ensure there was no physical contact between visitor and prisoner. The guard who had watched her being patted down stood in the corner of the room.

'No,' the woman on the other side of the Perspex demanded. 'She is an Australian citizen. I am her lawyer and I have the right to speak to my client alone. You can watch us outside from the camera.' Charlotte was impressed by how the woman exerted authority. The guard left, leaving them alone.

'Bravo,' Charlotte blurted out without thinking. 'Can you give me assertiveness training?' The woman smiled.

'I don't know how much time we will have, Charlotte. I doubt I've shooed her away for very long. My name's Amber and I'm from the Australian Embassy in Yangon. Are you OK?' Charlotte nodded. 'And Maiah?

'She's fine and in remarkably good spirits given our incarceration. What's happening outside today?'

'The military are continuing to tighten their grip on power. But on the other hand, those leaders who have not yet been contained, are calling on the general public not to recognize the military council or participate in its newly appointed government. Many people have been picked up, including Professor Tiell.' Charlotte took a deep breath and nervously sucked in her bottom lip.

'Is there anything you'd like me to do for you while I work to get you released? Tell your parents perhaps?'

'Absolutely no way. They don't know I'm in Myanmar and for the moment they don't need to. Please do not release my name.'

'Of course. Your response doesn't surprise me given

your objective for visiting the country in the first place.' So Amber knew she was an intelligence officer.

'There is one thing I need. There's a fashion show tomorrow tonight, if you can believe it and Maiah and I need to make our outfits today. So little time. I've already acquired several lovely pieces of satin on my sourcing trip. Can you ask Dang to drop them off today with all the thread and other materials I'll need?'

'Of course.' Amber waved at the camera and a guard came to collect her. Charlotte was returned to her dormitory where Maiah was waiting.

'What did you learn?' Maiah asked.

'That the military continue to arrest leaders from the National League for Democracy. Those who remain are calling for the resistance to continue. There are few leaders left who can speak out. Think about that.'

Charlotte made the decision to invest herself fully in preparations for the fashion show. It was an easy way to talk to all the women and to learn about the layout of the prison, the temperament of the guards and the daily pattern of life. With Maiah's help she also learnt more about the circumstances that had led to each woman's incarceration. Some had been involved in drug running or prostitution. Others were persuaded into criminal activities because of poverty. Charlotte felt compassion for them all.

At eleven o'clock she was again summoned by a guard to a visitors' room. Spread out across the table were the following items:

- Two short sleeved tops in gold and emerald green. They were identical in style and fabric to the *special shirts* that Maiah and Charlotte had been wearing when they arrived, which had now been confiscated.
- Four pieces of fabric. Charlotte only recognised two of these.
- Several spools of thread in varying colours.
- Two plastic containers of pins.
- Pack of multi-sized needles.
- Small scissors.
- Several packs of buttons to be covered with fabric.
- Three zips.
- Tape measure.

'Very pretty,' the guard said touching the fabric.

'Shall I make something for you?' Charlotte asked. The guard's face lit up.

'Come to the dining room in an hour and I'll measure you.' The guard helped Charlotte put all the items back into the large shoe box that they'd been delivered in. Charlotte immediately recognised that the two containers of pins were heavier than expected. She wondered what other surprises the box held.

Charlotte and Maiah carefully examined the contents of the box together. Charlotte already knew about the effectiveness of the fabric in the shirts in stopping a knife or a bullet. Two of the new pieces of fabric appeared to be made of the same material. This was confirmed when unsuccessful attempts were made to cut or tear it. The thread had been constructed of equally impenetrable material. Underneath a sponge inside the pin box was a layer of dark dust. From the smell, it appeared to be gunpowder. This would only be of use if there was a lighter somewhere in the pack. An examination of the pack of needles revealed a strip of red phosphorous on the back, leading to assume that several of the needles had a head containing potassium chlorate. The high number of buttons could have been used on twenty outfits. They must have a functionality beyond the obvious. But what was it? Their secret was revealed when one was dropped on the floor revealing a firecracker like effect. The small scissors appeared completely useless as they did not cut fabric. After Maiah opened and closed the scissors in quick succession multiple times, she inadvertently generated a power source which enabled the scissors to smoothly cut through the special fabric and thread.

The box was opened and examined carefully to see if there was a message from Dang secretly hidden inside one of the flaps. There was nothing. Maiah turned the box over and was aware that her fingers had touched something sticky. She put her fingers to her lips and immediately identified the taste of lime. The box was moved into the narrow ray of light entering the room from the tiny window above Charlotte's bunk. A message was now visible:

8:00pm tomorrow. North wall.

Charlotte went to great efforts measuring the guard for
her outfit, while Maiah chatted to her, asking questions
about her family and village. With all the measurements
obtained, work on making the outfits began. All the prisoners were excited and wanted to help, which was a
problem as Charlotte did not want anyone else touching
the fabric being used for their outfits. This problem was
overcome by Maiah asking two of the women to work
exclusively on the guard's outfit and for the rest to help
with the decoration of the stage. This would involve the
making of bows and flounces constructed from the left-
over fabric. This kept the women busy for several hours.
The warden made an unannounced visit and was
delighted with this hive of activity.

There was a buzz in the air over dinner that evening.
The fashion parade and the act of working on a project
together was building a strong sense of community
among the inmates. Maiah asked them how the event
would be run.

'How could we make it even better?' Charlotte asked
and Maiah translated. There was a lively discussion with
much laughter. As she didn't understand what they were
saying she watched and felt the joyful mood sweeping
across the group. And then she felt sad, worried that their
escape, if successful would jeopardise future events of this
kind. She also worried about using the explosives inside
the pin cases. What if someone was hurt? Charlotte
decided in that moment to abandon use of anything that
would cause harm. She was confident they'd find a way to
escape without the need to blast holes in walls.

The women were still whispering as Charlotte snug-
gled down into bed. The resident rat scurried across the

floor and a thin stream of moonlight gave the room an otherworldly feel. For the second night in a row, Charlotte drifted off to sleep thinking about Scott.

8

FASHION PARADE

There were several activities buzzing after breakfast. A few prisoners sewed sashes, marking each woman's home town or village on the fabric. Another group worked on music selection, while Maiah briefed the woman chosen to be the master of ceremonies. A further group decorated the stage and set out the chairs for the guards. Charlotte gave demonstrations on how to walk, turn and smile. There were giggles and dramatic gestures as each woman took their turn practicing their strut on the runway. Maiah then briefed the girls on thinking about the message they would like to share with everyone that evening. While each woman worked on their message or pitch, Charlotte walked around the prison complex to assess its vulnerabilities. The walls were formidable, topped with barbed wire and broken glass. There were cameras on every corner, way out of reach of interference from curious hands. The guards had a rostered walk around the jail every fifteen minutes, providing a very narrow window of time to work unseen. Charlotte returned to the room where final fittings were underway. She needed to make additional accoutrements for her and Maiah's outfits.

The evening meal was quickly consumed and the pans and plates were cleaned and put away. The fashion parade was scheduled to run from 7:00 until 8:00pm. At 6:45pm the warden and several guards arrived and were escorted to their seats and offered a cup of tea. There was orchestral music playing softly. Promptly at the top of the hour the master of ceremonies walked out from behind the curtains, and up the central runway. Charlotte had little idea what was being said, but by the look on the warden's face, gratitude was being expressed for this opportunity. A polite round of applause emanated from behind the curtains. The master of ceremonies then announced the first model, who came from the nearby village of San Hlan. She nervously walked up and back and then up the runway again. She paused for the applause and then shared what she would be doing in her family's fishing business when she went home. The next girl shared that she would improve her English so she could obtain a role in the tourism industry. Charlotte was next, saying that when she went home, she was going to hug her boyfriend. Her message was quickly translated into Burmese causing a ripple of laughter around the room. Maiah was next. She paused at the end of the runway for a moment before speaking.

'When I go home, I will continue the fight for democratic reform to ensure a fairer and better future for everyone in Myanmar.' There was a sharp intake of breath as all eyes focused on the warden, to see how she would react. She ever so slightly nodded, recognising the comment, and Maiah returned to join the other girls behind the curtain. The parade continued until each girl had walked the runway and shared their plan for what they'd do after their release. The concluding activity was a song sung by three girls with beautiful harmonies. As the song concluded the sound of saucepans banging outside the jail signalled that it was 8:00pm. The women walked onto the runway from behind the curtain and started stomping their feet in support. The warden stood up and raised her hands, indicating they needed to stop. She then looked among the women and asked, 'Where are Maiah and Charlotte?'

9

ESCAPE

Charlotte was pleased that no one had remarked on their unusual sashes or matching gloves. Having made their appearance on the runway, they knew they only had a small window of opportunity to escape. Most of the guards were in the main hall watching the fashion show. She had her fingers crossed that those watching the video monitors were asleep or distracted. As they entered the exercise yard on the north side of the complex, Charlotte threw a handful of the button firecrackers at the camera. At the sound of breaking glass, they made a run for the far wall. Charlotte joined their sashes together to create a lasso and rope to climb the wall. She lifted Maiah up on her shoulders and she was able to climb to the top of the wall and tie the barbed wire with strips of fabric that had been plaited together. The bullet resistant gloves helped shield her hands from the broken glass, but her bare feet were cut. A whistle from the other side was a sign that Dang was waiting. Maiah jumped, landing heavily on the other side of the wall as the sound of saucepans and rubbish bins being hit with force reverberated throughout the city. Charlotte knew that they would only have a minute until their absence was discovered. She climbed up the makeshift rope and gently traversed the barbed wire. As she pulled her leg over and looked back into the exercise yard, she could see the warden watching her. The woman raised her arm in a three fingered salute and Charlotte jumped to freedom on the other side.

Maiah had hurt her ankle on landing and was having difficulty walking. Dang and Charlotte carried her across the road while the clashing and banging continued. Two bikes were leaning against the fence.

'Too dangerous for the car,' Dang whispered. Dang propped Maiah on his cross bar and Charlotte rode the second bike. The night curfew was still in place, so they rode slowly, listening for the sound of military trucks. They pulled in behind the Tanintharyi Cultural Museum, on the road out of town, where Dang's truck was parked.

'Why aren't we staying at a safe house in Dawei?' Maiah asked Dang.

'Because today they broke into our offices and seized our computers and records. The people in those houses have had to flee, and to be honest I'm not sure where we should go. We need to get off the road as we draw attention to ourselves.'

'Do you know the way to San Hlan village?' Charlotte asked.

'Yes,' Dang replied. 'It's about thirty kilometres from here.'

'One of the women in the prison comes from the

village. She told us two things that were interesting. The first is that it's impossible for big trucks to drive down the narrow road into town. So the military cannot enter. Secondly, there's a large guest house at the end of town where foreigners can stay. It has a good view back to the village and the only road into town. I think it would be an excellent place to take shelter.'

They loaded the bikes into the back of Dang's utility, checked there was no traffic on the road and cautiously drove out from behind the museum to San Hlan. The road was indeed narrow and steep as it descended into the village. Multiple flickering lights revealed the location of twenty fishing boats anchored in the bay. The three of them were warmly welcomed at the guest house and given bandages and crutches. Charlotte suspected that Maiah's ankle was broken rather than sprained and would need professional attention. As she carefully bound the ankle, and attended to the cuts on Maiah's feet, she could hear the restful sound of monks chanting on the other side of the bay.

Charlotte woke with a fright the following morning. Someone was poking pins in her feet. She jumped out of bed ready to defend herself, to discover that one of the guest house puppies had pushed her door open in the middle of the night and had been chewing on her toes. She picked the scoundrel up and his tongue furiously lashed her face.

Maiah and Dang were sitting on the deck when Charlotte joined them.

'How's your ankle?' Charlotte asked. Maiah shrugged her shoulders. 'We need to get it looked at.'

'I don't think that will be possible,' Maiah replied. 'The generals will be watching the hospitals.' Charlotte pondered possible options and turned to Dang.

'Is the internet still down?

Dang nodded distractedly, looking out over the bay. He was watching a bird floating on the breeze and moving slowly towards land. Charlotte walked down the steps of the guest house and watched the drone land on the concrete platform. In a small box was another watch with a note.

Well done Charlotte. Call me. Teal

Charlotte secured the watch on her wrist and hit the call button.

'Hi Teal.'

'You OK?'

'I'm fine but Maiah has hurt her ankle. I'd like it to receive medical attention.'

'Will do. Get her across the border to safety today and I'll get a medic to her. Anything else?' Charlotte had so many questions, but it didn't seem like the time to ask.

'No. I'm good.'

'There's likely to be military on the road to the border. Make sure you have your fabric scouting story ready.'

'Will you be in Thailand when we arrive?'

'Hoping to be there tomorrow. Have a flight booked to

Bangkok tonight from Port Vila. Let me know when you've found somewhere safe to stop.'

'Will do.'

'Safe travels.'

Dang and Charlotte helped Maiah down the stairs of the guest house and into the Hilux. She grimaced in pain, but said nothing. Unfortunately, it was a bumpy drive out of the village and up the hill to the main road. This time Maiah could not contain her anguish and groaned each time the truck hit a pothole. As they crested the hill a ribbon of concrete ran out in front of them and Maiah's misery disappeared for an hour until they once again hit the rough, sandy track that was the main road to Htee Kee and the border. Charlotte's watch immediately started beeping. There were military vehicles using the road, driving slowly to avoid slipping off the edge into the river gorge. The dust made it difficult for the troops to see inside their vehicle. They stopped at a state checkpoint and found themselves sandwiched between a military truck in front and one behind. Dang had the music blaring and with the two bicycles prominent in the back of the utility, that provided a level of explanatory cover.

After ten minutes they were waved on and continued the journey across several precarious timber bridges. Two hours later they made it to a town called Myitta on the map. Calling it a town was generous as it appeared to consist of one restaurant, where all motorists stopped for a break. Dang spotted the group of cyclists that Maiah and Charlotte had cycled with a few days previously. They joined their table and were greeted like old friends. The soldiers also stopped to eat at a table on the other side of the restaurant.

'What happened to your ankle?' they asked Maiah.

'I fell off my bike.'

'Bummer. At least it was at the end of your trip.'

'Where are you headed?' Charlotte was asked.

'Thailand, obviously. With the internet down we've not been able to book accommodation. We'll have a look once we're on the other side of the border.'

'There are spare rooms at my guest house if you're interested,' Chris, the leader of the cycling tour said.

'Really? That would be fantastic. Where is it?' Charlotte asked.

'Near Huay Plu. About ninety minutes from the border.'

'Great. Accepted with thanks. And we'll travel with you as a part of your convoy.' A hush fell across the group as several soldiers walked past their table on the way to their truck.

'Isn't this coup terrible?' one of the women from the cycling group whispered. Her partner put his finger to her lips and they all took a nervous sip from their drinks. They scrutinized the soldiers as they climbed back into the military truck and were surprised when they turned left and headed back along the road in the direction of Dawei.

'Only three hours to the border with Thailand,' Chris announced as he picked up his water bottle and walked back to their utilities. He glanced at the body of their truck, with the bullet holes and turned to Dang. 'I see you had quite a few stones ricochet off your body during your trip.' Dang looked at him carefully.

'Yes. We're definitely looking forward to being on smoother roads.'

It felt safer driving behind two other vehicles carrying bicycles. All three vehicles continued their slow and slippery slide to Htee Kee. When they were thirty minutes from the border, Chalotte's phone emitted a warning beep and a large military truck appeared in the windscreen mirror. Dang said nothing, but his eyes flickered across the road in front of him as he considered their options. Charlotte quickly sent a text to Teal.

Military on our tail. Help requested.

No one spoke as they continued with their slow convoy to the border. Road conditions made it impossible to drive at more than fifty kilometres an hour. Fifteen minutes after the military first appeared in the mirror, they could hear the sound of a driver impatiently honking a horn. Charlotte and Maiah turned around and could see another utility overtaking the truck, the driver shouting abuse. Once in front of the military truck, the utility began driving in a zig zag pattern, slowing their speed and allowing the convoy of cyclists to move further ahead. As they increased their distance from the men in dark green, they could hear shouting and the explosion of tear gas. All three drivers put their foot on the accelerator, while their passengers grabbed the doors and each other as the vehicles rumbled to the border.

Htee kee was a small and uninspiring town, devoid of people and with a few ugly casinos under construction for the benefit of Thai gamblers. They thankfully arrived alone. Dang and Charlotte carried Maiah into immigration control and they all crossed their fingers that they'd soon be crossing the six kilometres of no man's land which preceded entry into Thailand. As they emerged with their passports duly stamped, they could feel the vibrations of heavy vehicles approaching. The three utilities drove quickly to a check point a hundred metres down the road. On the hill behind them, they could see that two military trucks had stopped and the soldiers were watching them. With a wave from a border guard they drove onto a relatively-smooth, concrete road traversing *terra nullius,* more commonly known as no man's land. Charlotte relaxed a little and looked at Maiah who was deep in thought. Something was on her mind.

Fifteen minutes later, they were through Thai immigration and back in their respective vehicles, on their way to the guest house in Huay Plu.

Charlotte texted Teal.

> *Back in Thailand. Arriving at guest house in 90 minutes.*
> *Please send medic. Coordinates follow.*

It was surreal being back in a country where everybody was going about their normal day to day lives. Finally feeling safe, Charlotte slept in the vehicle and didn't wake until a dog barked, welcoming them to the Hidden Holiday House at Huay Plu.

10

HUAY PLU

The sun was setting as they parked their utilities. Charlotte walked down to the river's edge at the bottom of the garden and took a seat on the pontoon. Large swathes of the plant called morning glory drifted by and egrets swooped above, returning to their favourite trees. It felt so calm and for the first time in over a week, Charlotte felt safe. She turned on her phone.

Message from Miranda. *So? Are you super chilled?*

Message from her mother. *Is it over? Interested to hear about the experience.*

Message from Mason. *Miranda and I have decamped from Krabi to Bangkok. Fab city. Want a bit of adventure before you go home? Join us.*

Message from Scott. *Loving Port Vila. Will be captaining a fantastic vessel in the practice race to Bundaberg. V.*

excited. Nearly as much as by the thought of being with you again. I'll call once we get close to an Aussie signal tower.

'Charlotte,' Dang called out from the house. 'There's someone here.' Charlotte slipped her phone in her pocket and walked back through the beautiful garden to the house. Maiah had her leg up on a chair and it was being examined by someone familiar.

'Well, Dr McDonald. Who'd have thought.'

Diane McDonald worked for Médecins sans Frontières, known in English as *Doctors without Borders*. That was the role as described when people asked. Like Charlotte, she also was on call to undertake other assignments as required. When Charlotte had been kidnapped by a criminal called The Monk the previous year, Diane McDonald was the medic on the evacuation team who attended to her leg injury. And a further curious twist in their relationship was that Diane's mother was the second wife of Charlotte's grandfather.

'So how do you know each other?' Chris asked.

'You know Australia. Small population. Everybody knows everybody,' Charlotte replied, supressing a smile.

'Where've you been?' she asked Diane.

'Most recently, I was working on a medical ship off Mawlamyine and later San Hlan.'

'Ah. I think I saw your ship from the roof of our hotel in Mawlamyine. And if you were not far from San Hlan, I'm guessing you sent the drone.'

'Guilty as charged.'

'Thank you. That watch was a life saver. And what are

your recommendations for our patient?' Charlotte asked, directing the focus back to Maiah.

'The ankle is broken and needs to be kept still, in this cast and elevated. This looks like an extremely suitable place for rest.'

'For how long?'

'A week would be good.'

'That's not possible,' Maiah replied. 'I need to go back to Myanmar.'

'I give the advice; I don't enforce it. The decision is yours, but your ankle needs to heal or it will be permanently damaged.'

'Thank you, Doctor.'

Charlotte walked Diane out the back of the guest house to the car park and was surprised at her mode of transport.

'A motorcycle, Diane? And you're a doctor.'

'We all need to live a little dangerously,' she said as she flicked back her ginger bob, put on her helmet and revved the engine. Charlotte waited until the bike had turned the corner at the end of the lane before returning inside.

'What's the news?' she asked Dang.

'President Biden has said that the US government will impose sanctions on those responsible for the coup.'

'Yay,' Charlotte and Maiah called out high-fiving each other. 'Further,' Dang continued, 'Biden has said that the sanctions will focus on military leaders and their family members along with their business interests. The US will also enforce strong export controls. The people of Burma are making their voices heard and the world is watching.'

'Can't you see that I've got to get back? Momentum is building to force them to stand down. I have to go to strengthen the resistance.'

'But if you're arrested again?'

'Yes. That might happen but I think they're afraid of me. Today, we were not being chased with the intention of containment. I'm sure they were chasing us to make sure we crossed the border. We've done exactly what they wanted.'

'I know Teal won't be happy. She wants to keep you protected, like a plant in a glass house, so that when the environment is more conducive, you can safely return home and flourish.'

'But we won't get there if we don't push hard now.'

'Can you think about it overnight?'

'Of course. But no promises.'

Charlotte cast her eyes out across the river before looking back to Maiah.

'I have an idea for how you can get your message out into the international spotlight as well as to your own people. Let me make a call.'

Mason loved the idea and said he'd be down first thing the following morning to interview Maiah. Miranda also expressed delight at visiting the resort.

'More a comfy guest house than a resort,' Charlotte corrected. 'I'll explain once you get here.' Maiah thought an interview with a well-known publication was a good idea, although she thought that *The Economist* would have been a better target than the magazine *Hello*.

'I agree. But I don't know anyone working for *The Economist* who's available to interview you tomorrow morning.'

'Thank you for arranging this,' said Maiah. 'Can I ask

you both to help me to my room now, please? I need to give my ankle the rest the doctor recommended. And I need to think about what I want to say to the people of Myanmar, as well as those who are influential in the broader community.' Again, it was easy to see why she'd been identified as a leader.

Charlotte closed the door to Maiah's room, and pulled a Singha beer from the fridge before walking down to the pontoon. Two cyclists were gently moaning on the terrace as they were given a Thai massage. One of the masseuses looked up at Charlotte.

'Tomorrow?' Charlotte whispered. The woman nodded while continuing to dig her thumbs into the groaning recipient's shoulders. The moon was clearly visible through the cloud free sky. As had been her habit most evenings at this hour, Charlotte's thoughts turned to Scott.

'Bye. See you next year. Thanks again, Chris.' Charlotte could hear the cycling troop departing for the airport as she came down the stairs for breakfast the following morning. Maiah was already seated at the communal table with her leg resting on a pillow. She was diligently writing on a sheet of paper. She looked up at Charlotte and smiled, noticing that she was carrying several colourful sarongs and tops.

'And you have clothes for my interview too?'

'Indeed, I do. I plan ahead. Do you have a preference, or you can wear them all?'

'Where were they made?'

'In Hpa-an.'

'I'll wear them all. Make sure we get the journalist to mention the factory in the article.'

'I will and here he is. Morning, Mason.' She waved at her friend tentatively walking into the central terrace. 'Did the taxi driver have any difficulty finding us?'

'Yes. This little hidey hole is certainly off the grid, Miss Wyatt.'

'And such a lovely place for a retreat,' Miranda added walking over and giving her best friend a hug. 'I think that you probably need another week though C. You don't look that rested,' Miranda whispered in her ear.

'Agreed. I do need more tender treatment, which is why I've arranged for us all to have a relaxing massage this morning.'

'I'm confused. I thought your mindfulness retreat was near Mae Sot?' Miranda commented.

'Well, it was. But I got expelled for talking to your brother on the phone. Lucky to be able to get in here at short notice.'

'You lovebirds,' Miranda cooed while gently punching her friend in the arm. Maiah was watching the exchange between the friends with amusement. Miranda introduced herself and asked what happened to her ankle.

'I fell off a ...'

'Bike,' Charlotte chipped in before Maiah could answer.

'You were lucky to be here in Thailand when this awful coup happened. Dreadful business. Myanmar's not too far from here is it?'

'No. Not too far.'

'When do you think you'll go back?'

'Today. I'm going back today.'

'Isn't that dangerous?'

Maiah hesitated before responding.'Sometimes in life you have to take a risk.' Charlotte's watch beeped indicating the arrival of a message. She read it, excused herself and walked down to the water's edge to call Teal.

'Hi Teal. How was the flight?'

'Fine. I'm currently in the immigration queue at the airport and will get a car directly to Huay Plu once I'm through. Should be there in two hours.'

'Look forward to seeing you. Umm, and,' Charlotte hesitated.

'Yes?'

'I'm not sure that Maiah will be here when you arrive.'

'Not acceptable. You need to change her mind. For her own safety and for the future of her country.'

'Understood.' Charlotte walked back to the main meeting room where Mason was in full interview mode with Maiah.

'And finally, what do you want to say to the people of Myanmar?'

'That only together will we be strong enough to build the democratic future we demand.'

'Brilliant,' Mason replied. 'Let's get a few photos now in these snazzy outfits.' It was funny how Mason's Australian accent had been infused by English colloquialisms. Charlotte and Miranda helped Maiah to change outfits and to move to different locations. There were some lovely backdrops to choose from, including several walls of flowers. Charlotte looked at her watch.

'Got everything you need, Mason?' He nodded. 'Good. Because Maiah and Dang need to get going.' Maiah picked up on the urgency in Charlotte's voice and sent Dang to get her bag. She looked at Charlotte and gestured for her to come closer. She wrapped her arms around her and held her close.

'Thank you,' she whispered. 'Hope you won't be in too much trouble.' Charlotte shrugged her shoulders slightly before warmly shaking Dang's hand.

'Good luck with getting more books into Myanmar. It's been wonderful to meet such a motivated librarian.' For a moment they just stood there. Charlotte leant forward and gave Maiah the watch Teal had given her. 'You might be able to use this.' She then raised her arm with the three fingered gesture.' Maiah and Dang saluted back.

'You know I'm resisting the urge to say...' Charlotte began.

'All for one and one for all,' Dang completed her sentence.

Charlotte watched Dang's bullet-riddled utility drive down the lane and turn right. As they departed, another vehicle arrived, carrying the masseuses that had been booked the previous day.

'Massage time, Miranda.'

'I have so many questions and so much to tell you...'

'Later my friend. Pamper time first.'

Charlotte and Miranda lay down on the mats and closed their eyes and waited for the magic of the masseuses' hands on their bodies. There was a breeze blowing up the river, and with the knowledge that her assignment was over, Charlotte relaxed and drifted off to sleep. Miranda looked across at her friend and wondered why she was so tired.

∽

When Charlotte woke up an hour later, Miranda was not lying on the other mat. She rolled over and was startled to see Teal standing beside her mat, glaring at her.

'You let her go,' she said accusingly. 'My instructions were very clear.'

'I don't remember obedience being one of the core competencies required when you recruited me.'

'I'm not pleased with your attitude.'

'Then you shouldn't have recruited me.'

'Yes. So it seems.'

'It wasn't my role to contain her. Myanmar is her country and the decision to go back was hers alone.'

'She may disappear again; she may even be killed.'

'Maiah knows that. It's her choice. She'd rather die fighting for democracy than stay in the safety of another country. The risks in returning were very clear to her.'

Teal crossed her arms and walked a few steps away, deep in thought. For a moment neither of them spoke.

'There is something good that has come out of this,' Charlotte said. 'I was able to get her an interview with a leading magazine so her message about what's happening in Myanmar and what support is needed, can be transmitted widely to the international community. And perhaps, with your support and the assistance of some of those drones, we can drop her messages across the country. I think that's an entirely acceptable outcome.'

'What did she say in the interview?'

'Let me find the reporter. Mason was working out of a games room out the back. 'Can you show Teal the notes from your conversation with Maiah?' Mason hesitated, then slowly turned his computer screen around. Teal slowly read his transcript.

'Yes. This is good. Can you send it to me?'

'As soon as it's published,' he replied promptly.

'Of course. Here's my card.' She looked from Mason to Charlotte. 'Well, there's no need for me to stay any longer. I'll get back to Bangkok. Thank you for your service.'

'I know it's normal to say *my pleasure*, but that would be a lie,' Charlotte replied.

Teal blinked and looked at her critically.

'I see you've lost your second watch.'

'It's gone to a better place.'

'You're an expensive asset.'

'I think a valuable asset was the expression you were looking for.'

'Touché,' Teal replied with a smile. 'À la prochaine. See you next time.'

'Perhaps,' Charlotte said offering Teal a handshake, and consciously choosing not to respond in French. She also did not accompany her to the car park nor watch her depart. Walking back inside the guest house, she was confronted by an excitable Miranda, throwing her hands around.

'Can we talk now? I have so many questions and things to tell you?'

'Miranda! Is that an engagement ring on your finger?'

'Yesssss. And I'm so happy.'

'When did this happen? What wonderful news. Tell me everything. Well perhaps not *everything*. You know what I mean.' The girls immediately barrelled down into their familiar scrum.

'And of course, I want you to be my bridesmaid.'

'Yikes. Of course. I'm so excited for you both. When do you plan to get married?'

'As soon as possible. Mason wants to get back to work

in London and take me with him as Mrs Miranda Murray. Doesn't that have a lovely ring to it?'

'Yes. It has a distinct rhythm to it.' Charlotte started humming. 'Could even be a song title. Certainly, it has a strong brand potential, like 3M. So, when and how did this all happen?'

'We had such a lovely time together at Krabi. As we got to the end of the holiday, we started having those conversations around when we'd see each other again. You know. We were both sad to think we'd be back living on the other side of the world from each other.' Miranda sighed, shaking her head. 'Mason suggested we go back to Bangkok early, for a special end of holiday celebration. He booked us into the Banyan Tree Hotel, which was fab, and then booked a table at their rooftop restaurant. It's amazing up there C. It's called Vertigo, you should seriously check it out. Then he sent me off in a tuk-tuk to buy something special to wear and he went down to Chinatown to check out rings. Except that I didn't know that, of course. The restaurant had the most spectacular view I'd ever seen, but Mason told me he only had eyes for me. Yes, I know it was corny, but I LOVED it. And as we sipped champagne, with clouds so close I could tickle them, he proposed. And I said yes. And I shrieked. And all the people at the nearby tables started clapping. And the waiter brought me a rose. And now I'm a fiancée and am soooo happy.' Miranda beamed. Charlotte loved soaking in her friend's joy.

'That story is good enough to bottle. I'm thrilled for you both. Congratulations. What did your parents say?'

'Not told them yet. Mason wanted to speak to Scott first, which has been impossible while he's racing across the ocean. Hopefully today, we'll be able to tell everybody the good news.'

'I wonder if they have champagne here?' Charlotte said, looking around to find someone she could ask.

'That would be pretty unlikely at a retreat, C. We can have a drink at the airport tonight,' Miranda responded.

'Yes of course. How silly of me.' She looked at her wrist and realised she no longer had a watch. She'd need to shake that habit. She turned on her phone to check the time. They had three hours to kill until they needed to leave for the airport.

'Wanna take a kayak up the river?' Charlotte asked Miranda.

'Yes please.'

'You'd better take that beautiful ring off and slip into something a bit more suitable then.' When Miranda left to change, Mason walked over to Charlotte with a package.

'Hey congratulations Mr Murray. Fab news.' She kissed him on the cheek.

'Thank you.' He passed the package to her. 'Maiah asked me to give these back to you with her thanks.' Charlotte looked inside the paper bag to see the three outfits she'd given Maiah to wear for the photo shoot. 'Dead lucky I'd say that you're both exactly the same measurements, although I'm sure you're taller.' He paused before continuing. 'Maiah told me to make sure I included the name and contact details for the factory that made these outfits in my article. She said that you'd be able to provide these details. So what I've been asking myself is, why would you have knowledge of a fabric manufacturing site in Myanmar?'.

'OK. So, I may have snuck across the border to do a bit of fabric sourcing, between retreats.'

'And I'm guessing that you also met Maiah, *between retreats*?'

'That would be correct.'

'And can I also assume there's a fantastic back story to how you met Maiah and one day you'll give me all the details in an exclusive interview?'

'That would also be correct, Mason.'

'Yay,' he replied fist pumping the air.

'What are you two talking about?' Miranda asked. Before either could reply, their conversation was interrupted by message alerts on their phones. They were from Scott. Mason called him before Charlotte had finished reading the message he'd sent her.

'Ahoy matey. Did you win? What does 'nearly' mean? And you didn't get seasick with all that? What's been happening here? Not too much. Well – apart from me asking your sister to marry me and her saying yes.' Scott's joy at the news could be clearly heard, even though the phone was not transmitting on speaker mode. 'Yes, yes,' Mason continued. 'She's here with me now.' He handed the phone to Charlotte. 'Strangely he'd like to speak to you.' Charlotte walked down to the river's edge.

'Hello there,' she said softly.

'So, there's going to be a wedding.'

'Isn't it wonderful news?'

'Sure is. I'm looking forward to it, but not nearly as much as I am to seeing you.'

'Me too,' she whispered.

'You still OK to do a quick turnaround in Brisbane and to hot foot it up to Hamilton Island?'

'Yes.'

'Great news. You should pass the phone over to the bride-to-be or I'll be considered a thoughtless brother. See you in a couple of days.'

Charlotte passed the phone to the very excited Miranda and listened to her friend share her joy.

'Yes. Yes. We're calling Mum and Dad next. We wanted to make sure we had the best man and bridesmaid roles confirmed before we did. Hamilton Island, eh? Not too shabby. Just make sure you're back in plenty of time for fittings. You'll have to wear a suit.' Charlotte smiled imagining Scott's feigned objections. By the time Mason and Miranda had called their parents, friends and various relatives there was no time for kayaking.

11

DON MUANG

It was quiet at the airport. BBC news was broadcasting updates from Myanmar. The situation had worsened with armoured vehicles now on the streets in several cities. A UN Special Rapporteur had been tweeting about late night raids; mounting arrests; the removal of rights; the ongoing shut down of the internet and of military convoys entering communities. He defiantly expressed support for the resistance movement and warned the generals that they would be held accountable. Charlotte wondered if the generals cared. A statement had been signed and released by the EU, US and UK, saying;

> We call on security forces to refrain from violence against demonstrators, who are protesting the overthrow of their legitimate government.

It was now known that Aung San Suu Kyi was under house arrest and five journalists were among those arrested. Public rallies were popping up in smaller towns and being led by a youth movement in Myanmar. There was no mention of Maiah Thar Khin, but Charlotte recognised the young girl wearing a mask and leaning on crutches to address the crowd. Charlotte sighed, mentally crossed her fingers and reflected on how lucky she was to have met this emerging leader. Her phone rang, interrupting her reverie.

'Hi Mum. How are you?'

'We're good. How was the retreat?'

'To be honest Mum, I'm rather pleased the experience is over.'

'That's not what I was expecting to hear you say.'

'Me either. Still, I learnt a few things about myself. And speaking about learning new things, guess who's getting married?' Charlotte could hear her mother's immediate intake of breath.

'Who?'

'Miranda and Mason.' There was a split second of silence.

'Lovely news. When's the big day?'

'Soon. Well, as soon as they can arrange it. Mason needs to get back to work in London and wants to get married before he goes.'

'Are you going to be making the wedding dress?'

'Goodness, I haven't been asked, and to be honest, the short time frame would make that pretty that challenging, particularly as I'm going to fly to Hamilton Island on Friday to chat with a couple of retail stores.'

'Don't throw yourself back into work so quickly, Charlotte. Take a break. Spend a few days with your parents.'

'OK. So, full disclosure here Mum. It won't be entirely a business trip. I'm also meeting up with Scott.'

'You two have certainly been spending a lot of time together.'

'Yes, we have,' Charlotte replied. She knew her mother was fishing for more information. That would have to wait.

'Well. Your dad and I are very much looking forward to having you home. And I must say we were relieved you were safely in Thailand and not in Burma with all that trouble going on. Dreadful stuff.'

'They're calling our flight now Mum. gotta go. See you tomorrow.' Charlotte rang off and slipped the phone into her pocket, feeling a little guilty at lying by omission. Still, this was one competency she was getting better at.

'Charlotte,' a familiar voice called out. Teal, of course.

'Fancy seeing you here.'

'I was hoping to catch you. I now know that an apology is in order. I've had a long chat with Maiah, who made it very clear that there was nothing that you could have said or done to keep her in Thailand. Further, she commended you for the way you acted throughout the time you were together. And I am particularly grateful that you gave her the watch. We've been able to learn what's going on in Myanmar and to take steps to keep her safe. I hope you will be open to accepting my apology.'

'Accepted,' Charlotte replied.

'Thank you. That your flight to Brisbane?' she asked pointing at the display board.

'Yes. Looking forward to being home in ten hours. And yourself. Where are you headed?'

'Back to Vanuatu.'

'Enjoy your trip.'

'We both know that's unlikely.' Charlotte smiled and offered Teal her hand. She shook it warmly, smiled, turned and walked along the concourse. Charlotte looked up at the display board and could see that passengers flying to Brisbane were now being invited to wait in the departure lounge. Miranda and Mason were already there.

'It's been one heck of a trip, hasn't it, C? What was the most memorable moment for you, apart from learning that we were getting married?'

'Let me see,' she said, dramatically tapping her index finger on her lower lip.

Charlotte remembered Scott's kiss as they said goodbye ten days ago. She remembered meeting and mistrusting Dang, before she discovered his motives. There was the confusion waiting in a café in Mae Sot for a contact who never arrived. There was watching the sun set over the sea from Kyaik Lan Pagoda in Mawlamyine and mistakenly thinking that her first assignment had finished. Then there was the cruise on the old fishing boats to Kyaikkhami, and cycling in the oppressive heat to Thanbyuzayat. And there was the car chase as they drove to Dawei with bullets rushing by. But of course, she couldn't forget Maiah's passionate speech, or being arrested, meeting the other prisoners, breaking out of the jail in Dawei and then running for the border.

'I think now, right now will be the most memorable moment when I look back. There's always such a pull, a powerful wave of emotion, when you're going home.'

EPILOGUE

Sharks were circling the yacht. Scott thought this amusing as there were also sharks aboard. Humour was his go-to-strategy when under pressure. How did he not see trouble coming?

THANKS FOR READING

I hope you enjoyed reading *Missing in Myanmar*. The book was written in real time when the military coup started on February 1 in 2021. The story, which is fiction, was influenced by the coup and by a cycling tour I'd undertaken twelve months earlier called *The Soft Nut Bike Tour of Burma*. (Find the book online and you'll discover my real name).

I'd love to know what you thought of *Missing In Myanmar* if you have the time to pen me a few lines. I get a kick out of listening to and chatting with readers.

Below are my contact details and social media hangouts.

- **Email me** at janeellyson@gmail.com and I'm also on,
- **Twitter** @janeellyson1– if you're a tweeter
- **Facebook** https://www.facebook.com/jane.ellyson.7 and

- **Pinterest**
  https://www.pinterest.com.au/janeellyson/pins/and
- **Instagram**
  https://www.instagram.com/janeellyson/

If you enjoyed the story, please tell your friends and write a review online. You can do this on Goodreads
    https://www.goodreads.com/author/show/
17708285.Jane_Ellyson
    or wherever you bought the book.

The sequel to *Missing in Myanmar* is *Nonsense in the North*. It is a thriller-romance set in North Queensland, Australia. If you're on my mailing list, you'll receive advance notice of its publication, which is planned for August 2021.

    https://janeellyson.com/

I've provided the prequel to Over Byron Bay, called Boy from Bangalow in the following pages. It's where the series started and was written because of reader feedback that they wanted to know more about Melissa and Andrew's relationship at university.

Happy reading,

Best
    Jane

BOY FROM BANGALOW (PREQUEL TO OVER BYRON BAY)

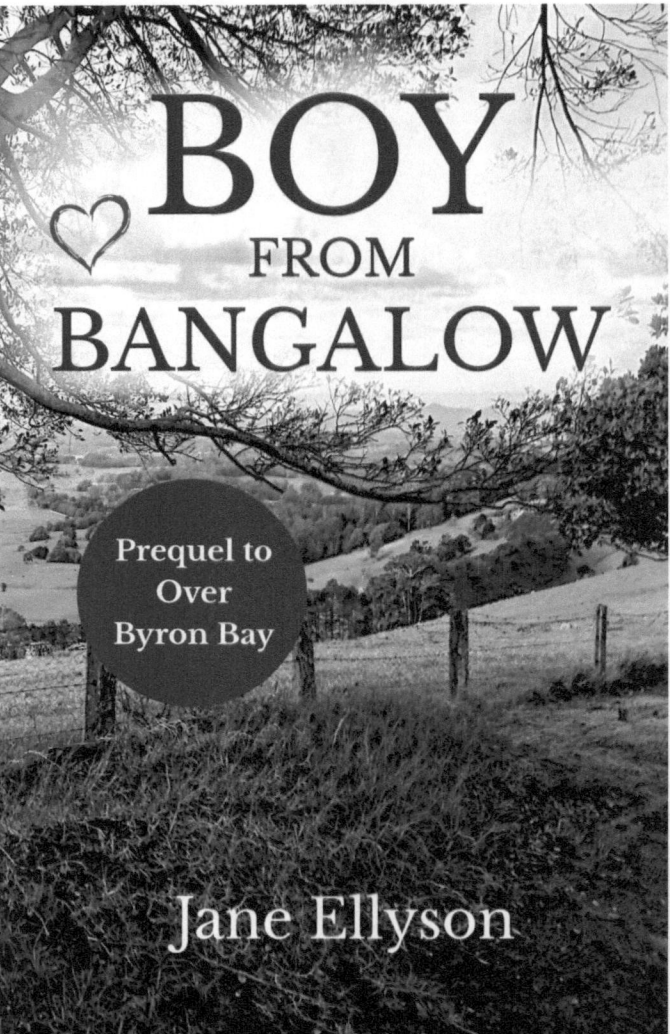

Family Tree

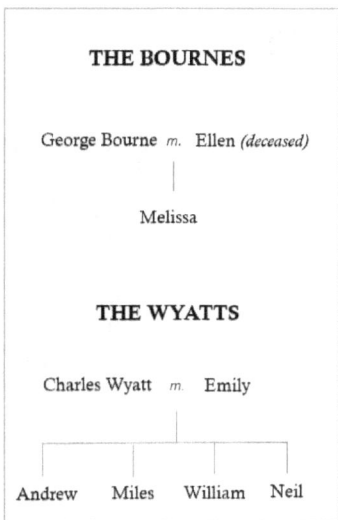

THE BOURNES

George Bourne *m.* Ellen *(deceased)*

Melissa

THE WYATTS

Charles Wyatt *m.* Emily

Andrew   Miles   William   Neil

Map: Ballina to Brisbane

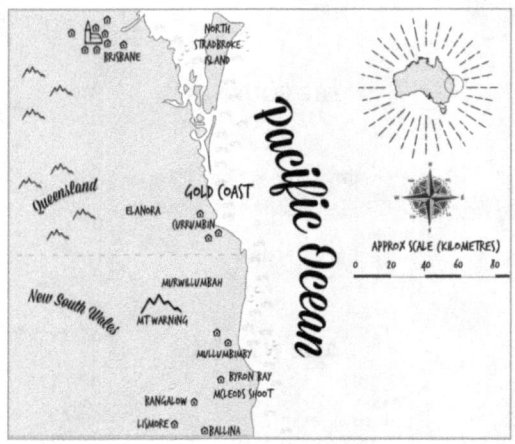

I. CONVERSATION IN THE CAFÉ

'A penny for your thoughts'. Startled, Melissa glanced up to see the familiar face of a neighbour.

'Ah the boy from Brisbane is back.'

'You mock me. I'll always be the boy from Bangalow.' She smiled.

'Haven't you taken up rowing and decided to study law? Both decisions influenced by that posh boarding school in Brisbane?'

'Both pursuits will enable me to live a comfortable life. I'll get to spend time on the water, (which I love),' he declared with emphasis, 'right the wrongs of the world and one day drive a Beemer.'

'I see.'

'And you? What are you studying?'

'Art and design.'

'Ah that's the reason for this,' he said tapping the book of landscapes open in front of her while sitting down uninvited on the small bench. He squeezed close to her as and she regarded him carefully. He smelt of freshly laundered washing. She looked into his smiling eyes, a little unnerved.

'No, not really. This book is for another purpose. I'm creating a ruse to get Dad out of the house.'

'Ahh. How is he. It's been what, well over a year since your Mum passed?'

'Yeah. Eighteen months now and Dad's still a hermit. He rarely goes out and he won't let me give away Mum's clothes that are still hanging in their wardrobe. Conversations are limited to me and *Boy*. That dog is such a lifeline but Dad needs other adult, human company. His friends from the Uni have stopped calling so I thought I'd get him to come here to Lismore, which is why I signed up for this.' Melissa slipped a pamphlet across the table announcing The Great Debate between the faculties. 'I've been telling him I need support so he has to come.'

'I see. Cunning plan.'

'You coming?' she enquired.

'Indeed I am. I'll be sharing the stage with you, arguing the case that *the pen is indeed mightier than the paint brush*.' Melissa looked up at the ceiling, closed her eyes and gently shook her head.

'I should've guessed. Any opportunity to argue.' He smiled revealing a set of slightly crooked, pearly white teeth. 'Will your parents be coming?'

'They might do, particularly now that they know who I'm up against.'

'Would be nice to catch up with your Mum'.

'There you are,' came a sultry voice from the entrance to the café. A short-haired siren, sashayed across the room and sat down on Andrew's lap, a clear sign of ownership.

'Melissa, this is Simone.' That would be *Simone Number Seven* Melissa calculated.

'Hi Simone,' she offered in a deadpan voice while looking at Andrew.

'Come Andy. Let's go.' Simone stood and looked expectantly at him.

'Ok then.' He said as a sigh. 'All the best with your preparation.' Melissa nodded, her head ever so gently, acknowledging him.

'See you at the debate *Andy*', Melissa offered, biting her lip to hide a smirk.

'Good luck with getting your Dad to come. I'll ask Mum to drop off a few nectarines and have a bit of a natter. She's pretty good at cajoling people.'

'Ta. That'd be appreciated.' Simone tugged on his sleeve, he stood and put his arm loosely around her waist. Melissa watched them walk to the door. Andrew threw her a glance before following Simone down the steps. She turned another page in her book but looked up distract-edly, thinking about Andrew's latest girlfriend. She mentally noted the names of the other women Andrew has courted. There was *Angst ridden Anne*, *Mia the Model*, *Bookish Belinda* and *Inky Ingrid*, whose neck tatts made her more than a little scary. She'd not met either Zoe or Kalinda, who Andrew's mother described as well-mannered. (She was sure she was holding back on what she really thought if this was all she could say.)

Andrew's mother Emily had been a wonderful support for her when her mother was dying, often calling by with something fresh from Byron markets. And she always had time for a cuppa, when she needed some-where calm away from the house. Melissa didn't have to talk, which was good because she didn't want to. It was somewhere safe to sit while Emily chatted about what her four sons were up to. Andrew had joined a friend at boarding school in Brisbane, which was 170 kilometres away, so Melissa only saw him intermittently during the previous two years. With their families owning adjoining farms, she more frequently saw his brothers tending cattle. Her eyes returned to her book, her mother's book, which included sketches and paintings from her mother's home state of Maine. They'd been planning a family trip before her mother was diagnosed with cancer. At that moment she missed her mother terribly and tears filled her eyes. She discreetly wiped them away and returned to debate preparation.

II. THE GREAT DEBATE

It was raucous in Lecture room 4 on Friday evening. New graduates were decked out in costumes from the 19th century, playing out roles of prominent politicians, lawyers and artists. The great debate was the penultimate event in orientation week, so everyone was in high spirits. Melissa's eye's flickered to her father. He was suppressing a smile. He was back in familiar territory. He had finally taken the shirt she gave him for Christmas out of the wrapper and he looked good.

'George,' came a voice from the front row. It was Marty Gordon, a fellow lecturer from the science faculty.

'It's fairly clear which case you'll be supporting tonight.'

'No Marty, as always, I'll be objective and guided by the facts as presented.' His friend chortled.

'Good to see you George, and to know you've not lost your sense of humour.' He took the last seat on the end of the fifth row, still keeping a little distance from others.

The familiar *tat tat tat* of fingernails on the microphone preceded a wave of hushes across the room.

Everyone took their seat and turned their attention to the master of ceremonies, formally attired in her graduation gown and cap. Octavia Hildengard was a formidable woman. She was one of the first women to become Vice-Chancellor in Australia. Her intellect and wit were well known.

'Good evening and welcome. Wonderful to see all the costumes tonight. I appreciated the conversation with academic and former president of the United States Woodrow Wilson, on income tax policy and racial segregation.'

'Oh,' is whispered across the room.

'And it was lovely to chat with English painter Helen Allingham on how she chose her wonderful landscape subjects. Tonight's topic is a cheeky play on the well-known adage that *the pen is mightier than the sword*. Here at Southern Cross University, we leave the study of military strategy to our colleagues at the Royal Military College in Duntroon, Canberra, choosing to focus instead in many other areas including the arts and law. So, tonight we will hear arguments for and against the proposition that *the pen is mightier than the paintbrush*.

It's my pleasure to introduce the debaters whose arguments may challenge your thinking or entertain you. I've asked both speakers to provide me with personal insights that many others wouldn't know. Arguing for the affirmative is Andrew Wyatt. Andrew is a first-year student in the faculty of law. His ambition is to ensure fairness and equity for everyone. In terms of something personal, Andrew's family produces the best mangoes in Bangalow.'

'Onya Andrew,' comes a cry from a fellow student and Simone stands, enthusiastically clapping, prompting everyone else to join. When the clapping fades the Chair continued.

'Melissa is a first-year student in the faculty of art and design. Her ambition is to travel widely and use design to bring beauty to the everyday. Something personal about Melissa, her father produces the best lychees in the Northern Rivers Region.' Everybody laughed and some of the academic staff started cheering. George Bourne beamed. A wide grin erupted across Melissa's face. This evening has already delivered the value she'd hoped for. Now to get this darn debate done.

The Chair nodded to Andrew to take his position behind the lectern in the centre of the stage. He momentarily shuffled the papers, took a deep breath, looked up at the audience, paused for a moment, and then smiled. He has their undivided attention.

Madam Chair, students and guests.
    In my hand I hold a source of great power.

(Andrew holds up a pen)

This humble instrument can explain rights and obligations, creating a safer and fairer world for all. The written word can encourage civilised behaviour, facilitate consensus in disputes, and inspire political action.

Laws reflect the values of the society within which they exist, and with the power of the pen, these laws can evolve to echo changing values and aspirations.

These values reflect how power is organised, exercised and controlled. At their heart, our laws reject unfairness, support dignity and mercy and insist on equality for all.

These are just some of the reasons why the pen has such an influence on our society and why I am proud to advocate that the pen is mightier than the paintbrush.

But pens do more than write laws. They can also explain philosophy often written down in books such as The Bible, Plato's Republic, Marx's Das Kapital and Darwin's Origin of Species. Think of a book that has influenced you by the inspiration of the vision or the power of the argument.

With a pen we can also write love letters.

(Andrew pauses and a murmur erupts among the female members of the audience.)

For example, from Prince Albert to Queen Victoria.

(Andrew reads dramatically)

Dearest deeply loved Victoria, I need not tell you that since we left, all my thoughts have been with you at Windsor, and that your image fills my whole soul. Even in my dreams I never imagined that I should find so much love on earth.

Or from Orson Welles to Rita Hayworth

(Andrew reads slowly and gently)

... I suppose most of us are lonely in this big world, but we must fall tremendously in love...to find it out.

(Melissa looks at her father who is affected by the words.)

And finally, a love sonnet from Elizabeth Barrett Browning.

How do I love thee? Let me count the ways.

I love thee to the depth and breadth and height my soul can reach.

If this last line does not convince you of the power of words transcribed by the pen

(Andrew holds a pen up),

I'm not sure, what will.

Thank you.

Andrew returns to his chair to rapturous applause led by chants of *Andy, Andy, Andy* from Simone, and several other girls who are snapping photos on their phones. He looked across to Melissa and winks, infuriating her. When the clapping subsides, she walks purposefully to the lectern, grasped its edges, and held a power pose. She scanned the room, took a deep breath and counted to three.

> Madam Chair, lovers of learning, lovers of life, *(she paused)* lovers of love.

> It's true. A pen allows us to communicate, but only to communicate in one way, through the written language of the author. We're lucky that here in this auditorium we speak the common language of English which is the third most popular spoken language in the world behind Mandarin at number one and Spanish at number two.

> Did you know that there are 4,000 written languages and over 6,500 spoken languages in the world? A single language is useful when the one community speaks in the same voice – but when we take a broader view, a global view, what channel has a universal capacity to communicate meaning and emotion beyond the written word?

> *(She paused again for effect)*

> I propose that it is the paintbrush or indeed any form of the arts that provides a universal language, and that it's been this way since the very beginning.

> Think of the way indigenous communities here in Australia have shared their history over time. They've used oral storytelling and song as well as

visual communication through drawing and painting. With no written language, many depended for their very survival on maps of country with painted landmarks to remember where food and water could be located.

My learned colleague Mr Wyatt seems very interested in using the pen for the making of rules and the creation of order. He shared wonderful aspirations for what we want the law to achieve, but some laws from the past and even those in the present, have subjugated people. He shared moving passages of love and there are those in the room who've formalised their love in a marriage contract which of course was originally created to ensure that women would remain dependent and subservient after marriage. Many of course have gained the power to own and control property, to vote and to choose the direction of their lives. I think of wonderful American 19th century impressionist painter Mary Cassatt, who is represented in the room this evening.

(A girl in the first row, who is delighted at having been recognised, stood and curtsied to Melissa, pivoted, curtsied to the audience, and then retook her seat. Not missing a beat, Melissa continued.)

Apart from being a wonderful painter, Mary Cassatt was also a feminist who recognised that marriage would be detrimental to her career and that women should *be someone* and not *something*.

You know, for me, life *as a creative* is not so much about making the rules but about breaking them; of challenging the status quo to achieve those things that Mr Wyatt mentioned like fairness, equity and justice; but also to feel joy, to experience beauty and to come to understand the very nature of the human condition. This is what art gives us and this is *why the paintbrush is more powerful than the pen*.

The audience is stunned. Melissa confidently nodded at the Vice Chancellor and resumed her seat. An enthusiastic round of applause rose from the auditorium. Andrew clapped rigorously as well, and looked at her as he stood and walked across the stage, and again took his place behind the lectern.

My word Miss Bourne, I feel your passion. Don't you?

(He addressed to the audience)

This is the first time I've been introduced to your revolutionary inclinations. Bravo.

I feel I need to respond to your concerning comments about the contract of marriage. Marriage has evolved. It's true that historically in most cultures, married women had very few rights of their own, being considered, along with the family's children, the property of the husband; as such, they could not own or inherit property, or represent themselves. However, since the late 19th century, marriage has undergone gradual legal changes, aimed at improving the rights of the wife and the children of the marriage. It's now an institution in many but not all parts of the world, entered into freely with obligations and protections shared and with objectives for companionship, personal growth and love. We have not reached utopia and like all aspects of the law, it needs to be reviewed, tested and updated.

You know, I think of other revolutionaries like Alexander Hamilton who also studied law. He was a man born out of wedlock, orphaned as a child who grew up to become an American statesman, politician, legal scholar, military commander, lawyer, banker, economist and one of the Founding Fathers of the United States, who was active in ending the legality of the international slave trade. He demonstrated the power of the pen to bring positive change, enriching the lives of others.

Miss Bourne, your points about art being a universal language are well made. However, I urge caution. Paintings can be ambiguous, which is dangerous when clarity is needed. The meaning to one person may not be the same as the meaning to another, and in a world where we want fairness and equity, we cannot afford the uncertainty that comes from ambiguity.

In closing, the law affects every part of our lives and the pen that writes our laws provides certainty and a foundation for a civil society. A pen can also be the vehicle for the distillation of philosophy and for the communication of love.

(Andrew paused).

And for these reasons I strongly submit that the pen is indeed mightier than the paintbrush.

A raucous round of applause fills the great hall. Andrew returned to his seat and Melissa moved quickly to the podium. She waited for a moment for the noise to subside.

The time for speaking is over. I need to let the power of art *(she paused)* speak for itself.

(The house lights dimmed and a 1964 painting by Norman Rockwell appears on the projector. Melissa stood and looked at the images for ten seconds before returning to the audience).

It's moving isn't it? You may not know the back story but you can feel the fear and feel the prejudice.

This 1964 painting by Norman Rockwell of Ruby Bridges is considered an iconic image from the Civil Rights Movement in the United States. Ruby was just a six-year-old African American girl, on her way to School, an all-white public school, during the New Orleans' school desegregation crisis of 1960. Because of threats of violence against her, she was escorted by four deputy U.S. marshals. On the wall behind her, you can see written the racial slur "nigger" and the impact of a splattered tomato thrown against the wall.

And another example.

(Melissa clicked on the next slide. A post-impressionist painting from the 19th century called Fields of Roussilion by Renee Gandy is displayed).

(Melissa again paused giving the audience time to examine the image.)

It's beautiful, isn't it? You may not have been there but you can already smell the lavender.

A painting can be a thing of beauty, inspiring us to pick up a paintbrush or to get out of our chair and to travel the world. To see things not seen before, to experience new tastes, breathe in new scents and explore new feelings. And speaking of feelings ...

(Melissa clicked on the final image of a painting by Carolus-Duran – le Baiser)

(Melissa paused. There were ahs from the audience.)

Can you feel the love tonight? Isn't this a wonderful image? Made even more special by the knowledge that this is a self-portrait of French painter Carolus Duran – le Baiser with his wife as newlyweds from 1868.

So, you can put your pens away. No words are needed here. Indeed, the paintbrush provides a universal language for all. It can mount an argument without words. Communicate beauty, reveal complexity, and allow us to experience love.

The act of painting, not only helps to develop our critical thinking but enables us to interpret the world around us.

And importantly, art brings us joy. And for these reasons (she paused) the power of the paintbrush surpasses the power of the pen.

(House lights return).

'Bravo.' George Bourne cried out, already on his feet clapping. He's soon joined by Andrew's parents and many others in the surrounding rows. Melissa smiled and returned to her seat. Octavia Hildengard was clapping as well with a huge grin across her face.

'My word. I don't know about you, but I'm quivering. I do not envy the task in front of our judges. What wonderful orators. Please join with me in thanking again our debaters.' There are cheers from the audience with Simone and a few friends attempting unsuccessfully to start a Mexican wave across the room. 'While our judges confer, it's my pleasure to announce the runners up and winner of the best costume from the 19th century.' She opened an envelope. 'The second runner-up is Michelle Kwee for her Daisy Bates costume. Please come up here

Michelle to collect your prize. For those of you not familiar with this 19th century figure, Daisy Bates was an Australian journalist, welfare worker and lifelong student of Australian aboriginal culture.'

Photos were taken and the Vice Chancellor returned to the microphone.

'The first runner-up prize goes to Harry Leavon for his inspired interpretation of the Australian writer and bush poet, Henry Lawson. Come up here Harry. I wonder if you chose Henry Lawson because of the similarity of your names or because you wanted to try out that outrageous moustache?' Harry grinned, wiggled his moustache, and shook the Chairs hand, before taking his envelope, smiling for the photographer, and returning to his seat. 'And the winner of the best costume goes to Elizabeth Fleur for her portrayal of Dame Nellie Melba who was ...' At this point an operatic voice can be heard singing, *There's no place like home,* from the back of the room. A polite round of applause ripples across the room and the chatter fell silent while people listened to the singer. 'Please join with me in congratulating our winner Dame Nellie Melba, also known as Elizabeth Fleur.' A small girl with strong lungs, dark, tight curls squeezed under a tiny bonnet and wearing a long-sleeved dress with satin pinafore, climbs the steps to the stage to collect her envelope and to pose for photos with the Vice-Chancellor. More applause followed.

'Well everyone. I've just been given the judges verdict. I invite Andrew Wyatt and Melissa Bourne to come stand with me. I think you'd all agree that they have represented their respective faculties brilliantly this evening.' One of the judges walked on to the stage with two wrapped boxes, one much larger than the other. 'In announcing the runner-up, I know that I will be simultaneously announcing the winner. In reality there is very little distance between the two. So, without further ado, I declare the runner up in our Orientation Great Debate on the topic that *the pen is mightier than the paintbrush* is Andrew Wyatt. Andrew beams as though he has been announced the winner.

'Thank you everybody. That concludes the formal part of the evening.' A photographer signalled for Andrew and Melissa to join the Vice-Chancellor for a photo in front of the university coat of arms.

'Are your parents nearby?' the photographer asks. They both nodded and waved their parents over for a photo.

'Well done Mel,' Charles Wyatt offered before patting his son on the back.

'You were brilliant,' Emily Wyatt whispered to Melissa, 'and you weren't too bad either son,' kissing him on the cheek. George Bourne beamed and took his place in the line-up for the photo. Several snaps later, the photographer asked for photos just with the winner and runner-up.

'I want you to strike a defensive pose.' Melissa and Andrew pass their presents to their parents, who look on curiously. They stood close to each other and struck a position as though they are boxing. Andrew didn't blink as he looked into her eyes. She felt unnerved and was aware that her heart had started beating faster. 'And now I want a photo as though you have just made up.' Melissa proactively put her hand out, offering to shake his hand. He smiled accepting her hand and stepped closer towards her. The camera starts clicking. When the photographer put the camera back into their bag, Andrew held on to Melissa's hand.

'I don't think that you'll be using your gift very much.'

'Au contraire. For a lawyer in training, you make a lot of assumptions. Certainly, this is a writing instrument with which I can write down my dreams and my thoughts, and my aspirations and my fears. But you only see it in one way. It's also a thing of beauty. Look at the colour. Look at the lines. Look at the beautiful gold tip. This is a piece of art that will bring pleasure to my life, simply by being. It's also a relic and a connection to a time that's passed. I'll take pleasure from it in a number of ways. Unlike those paint brushes of yours that are unlikely to get wet any time soon.' Andrew raises his eyebrows.

'Now, who's making assumptions?' Melissa looks into his lovely smiling eyes again.

'Touché.'

'You done?' Simone called out to Andrew from across the room.

'He's all yours,' Melissa returns.

'See you round.' Andrew touched her softly on the elbow and then saunters across the room to join Simone.

'Ready oh slayer of the legal profession.'

She kissed her father on the cheek and looped her arm through his.

'You bet.'

III. NEW PERSPECTIVES

Melissa wakes the following morning to an unfamiliar noise. It's not the cows mooing in the home paddock, or the kookaburras laughing from the back fence. It's the wonderful sound of her father rustling about in the kitchen. He's out of bed early for the first time in months. Grabbing her dressing gown and slipping on her Ugg boots, she joins him.

'Tea's in the pot,' he says in the most wonderful, normal voice as though they had shared this ritual every day. 'And we're out of lychees. Can you go pull a few for brekkie?'

'Of course, Dad.' She swapped her sheepskin slippers for her RM Williams boots, picked up a small bucket and headed down the garden path to the row of lychee trees. As she pulled a dozen of the deep crimson fruit from the branches, her eyes detect movement three paddocks away. She smiled when she spotted the familiar red flannel shirt and returned inside, placing the bucket on the kitchen bench.

'I'll get something to eat later Dad,' she called out as

she headed to her bedroom to change. It's such a lovely day she reflected as she crossed the small bridge over Byron Creek. Two magpies were showing their offspring how to spread their wings in preparation for flight while three wallabies watched her carefully from their vantage point in the long grass. As she climbed the last fence separating the families' properties, she started laughing. Andrew looked up.

'So, you're coming to mock me again?'

'I did not mock you. I simply challenged your argument. Do not confuse the object with the subject.'

'I see you are keen to apply your new skills. Very commendable.'

'Will you be joining me? I have a spare paint canvas.'

'Not today,' she replied reaching into her backpack to pull out a notebook and her new pen. 'I need a different perspective today.'

'You probably also need sustenance. There's a coffee thermos, mugs, fresh bread and homemade mango jam in the picnic basket.

'Expecting me?' she asks softly.

Melissa's father watches them from the kitchen window and smiles. Turning to his dog he says,

'Come Boy. You can supervise me clearing out the wardrobe.'

REFERENCES

Elizabeth Barrett Browning

- https://poets.org/poem/how-do-i-love-thee-sonnet-43
- History of legal contract for marriage
- Browning, E. B. (2013). Sonnets from the Portuguese. Doubleday.
- Salmon, M. (2016). *Women and the law of property in early America*. UNC Press Books.
- https://www.fedcourt.gov.au/
- https://www.countryliving.com/life/inspirational-stories/g4061/famous-love-letters/
- https://japingkaaboriginalart.com/articles/facts-about-aboriginal-art/
- https://www.babbel.com/en/magazine/the-10-most-spoken-languages-in-the-world#:~:text=Chinese%20%E2%80%94%201.3%20Billion%20Native%20Speakers,spoken%20language%20in%20the%20world.

About studying law

- https://www.trin.cam.ac.uk/undergraduate/courses/law/why-study-law/
- https://en.wikipedia.org/wiki/The_Problem_We_All_Live_With

ABOUT JANE ELLYSON

Jane has a deep connection to the Far North Coast of New South Wales in Australia. Her great grandparents owned a farm a little way out of Byron Bay and her grandparents were long term residents of Mullumbimby. She currently lives at Possum Creek, not far out of Bangalow – well she would if she was real – rather than being the pen name of someone who would prefer to remain anonymous. This is her fourth novel in the Northern Rivers series. The fifth and final book in the series is based in Queensland Australia and is called *Nonsense in the North*. I had so much fun writing it. Details about this book and indeed all the books in the series follow.

www.janeellyson.com
janeellyson@gmail.com

BOOKS IN NORTHERN RIVERS SERIES

Over Byron Bay (Book 1 of 5)

Melissa Bourne and Andrew Wyatt were neighbours in the country town of Bangalow in Australia. Friends, good friends were all they'd ever been. This situation suited them both until Andrew found someone else. Surprised at her jealousy and with an international job offer in hand, Melissa left the country. She accepted a job offer in Boston, met Jonathan Brinkley, married and settled into life in the U.S.

Five years later she returns to Bangalow for a visit with her father, shortly after the death of Andrew's mother. The two meet briefly at the funeral, and the day before she flies back to Boston providing an opportunity to rekindle their relationship and to recognise that their feelings for each other go beyond friendship. Melissa returns to the States in turmoil.

A novel which will take the reader on an emotional roller-coaster ride.

SUBSTITUTE CHILD

DISCOVERY OF A BOTTLE PROMPTS A WHIRLWIND JOURNEY OF ADVENTURE, LOVE AND A SEARCH FOR IDENTITY

JANE ELLYSON

BOOK 2 OF 5

Substitute Child (Book 2 of 5)

A deckhand in France discovers a bottle with a letter inside. The bottle has floated all the way from Byron Bay in Australia to the south of France. The discovery prompts a whirlwind journey for Charlotte Wyatt into the world of paparazzi, European royalty and the criminal underworld.

Substitute Child is the story of a student travelling to the other side of the world to collect a bottle with a love letter to a brother she never knew and a journey to discover who she is and what she wants from her life.

WHERE'S JACK?

ROMAN ROULETTE

MISSING FRIENDS AND THE MAFIA CAUSE
MAYHEM IN THE MEDITERRANEAN

JANE ELLYSON

BOOK 3 OF 5

Roman Roulette (Book 3 of 5)

Unable to leave Rome due to an air traffic controller strike, Charlotte accepts an invitation to a party on a super yacht. A friend disappears and then Charlotte becomes an accidental stowaway as the yacht heads for Sicily. Inadvertently caught up in the international slavery trade and forced to choose between several unbearable options, Charlotte embarks on a bold plan to save the women captured by the Monk, and in doing so, to save herself.

Adventure/thriller set between Rome, Naples and Taormina in Sicily.

NONSENSE
⬥ IN THE ⬥
NORTH

SAILING, SMUGGLING, SPYING AND
AVOIDING SHARKS, SNAKES AND SPIDERS

JANE ELLYSON
BOOK 5 OF 5

Nonsense in the North (Book 5 of 5)

The Australian bush has a reputation for being dangerous what with snakes, spiders and stinging trees – and that's just the start of it.

A too-good-to-be-true sailing trip results in Scott's disappearance from waters near Hamilton Island in Australia. Now considered by police to be an integral part of an international drug smuggling operation, Charlotte relies on a sympathetic police officer and an aboriginal tracker named 'Nonsense' to travel deep into Cape Conway, to disrupt a drug exchange and to find her Scott, improving their chances of a happily-ever-after. All the while helping plan her best friend's wedding.

Adventure/thriller set in Queensland, Australia.

www.janeellyson.com

CHOICES, CHAOS AND COMING HOME

JANEELLYSON.COM

www.ingramcontent.com/pod-product-compliance
Lightning Source LLC
Chambersburg PA
CBHW030436120726
47903CB00003B/984